P9-DXN-082

THE GOBLIN'S PUZZLE

The Goblin's Puzzle

Being the Adventures of a Boy with No Name and Two Girls Called Alice

by Andrew S. Chilton

Illustrations by
Jensine Eckwall

Alfred A. Knopf
New York

THIS IS A BORZOI BOOK PUBLISHED BY ALFRED A. KNOPF

Visit us on the Web! randomhousekids.com

Educators and librarians, for a variety of teaching tools, visit us at RHTeachersLibrarians.com

Library of Congress Cataloging-in-Publication Data
Chilton, Andrew S.
The goblin's puzzle: being the adventures of a boy with no name and two girls called Alice / by Andrew S. Chilton ; illustrations by Jensine Eckwall. — First edition.
pages cm.
Summary: A boy, a goblin, a scholar, and a princess join forces to defeat a dragon, outwit a scheming duke, and solve a logic puzzle.
ISBN 978-0-553-52070-5 (trade) — ISBN 978-0-553-52071-2 (lib. bdg.) —
ISBN 978-0-553-52072-9 (ebook)
[1. Fantasy.] I. Eckwall, Jensine, illustrator. II. Title.
PZ7.1.C5Go 2016
[Fic]—dc23
2015013261

The text of this book is set in 12.25-point Apolline.

Printed in the United States of America
January 2016
10 9 8 7 6 5 4 3 2

First Edition

FOR MY MOTHER, MARY-DELL CHILTON,
WHO MADE EVERYTHING POSSIBLE

KINGDOM OF
WEST STANHOPE
MOUNTAINS OF FIRE
FARNHAM
THE LITTLE
DISMAL
THE GREA
DISMAL
ROYAL PALACE
MIDDLEBURY
CASTLE GEOFFREY
ROGGENHEIM
THE WESTERN OCEAN

THE SPINE
KINGDOM OF
EAST STANHOPE
KINGDOM OF
HIGH ALBEMARLE
TO MOSSGLUM
ALBEMARLE CITY
CASIMIR'S
VILLA
ALBEMARLE BAY
N
W
E
S

1

Bread, left untended, will steal itself, or so people liked to say. But the boy found that sometimes it needed help. He peeked in through the back door of the kitchen. Cook stood by the oven with her big wooden paddle, waiting for the baking to be done. The lines on her face made her mouth look like it was curving downward, even when she was not frowning. No matter how hungry the boy was, Cook would never sneak him a loaf. One of the kitchen girls might, but Cook could not know. She'd sooner thwack a slaveboy's backside with a kitchen spoon than part with a single crust.

Of all the kitchen girls, Brigitte was the softest touch. The boy caught her eye, but she shook her head a little. He gave her his saddest look. She nodded toward Cook. With her paddle, Cook was lifting cake after cake out of the oven. The boy sighed. A bit of bread could disappear, but cake would be missed. He studied the cake. It was studded with raisins, shot through with cinnamon and topped with a glaze of sugar. The boy sniffed deeply. The hollow ache in the pit of his belly awoke. His mouth watered, and his stomach churned.

At the back gate, a great black dog whined and pawed to be let in. Pajti was the master's best hunting dog and an accomplished escape artist. The boy went to the gate and said, "Pajti want some cake?" Pajti gave the boy a couple of suspicious sniffs. Then he wagged his tail and licked the boy's hand through the grate. The boy let him in and took him by the collar. He led Pajti to the kitchen door. "Pajti want some cake?" he whispered. Pajti whined and nuzzled the boy's face. For luck, the boy rubbed his father's ring, which he wore on a thong around his neck. Then he let go of Pajti's collar.

Pajti shot into the kitchen like an arrow. He knocked down a girl carrying a basket, and potatoes flew in every direction. Pajti bounded over the girl and up onto the cutting table. He snarled at Cook. Cook shrieked and dropped her paddle. Cakes soared through the air. Screaming kitchen girls dropped everything and ran from the room. Tables flipped over and dishes clattered to the floor.

Pajti dropped to the ground and bit into one of the cakes. Cook was not going to surrender her kitchen so easily. She was tough for an old woman. She grabbed her long iron spoon and waved it at him. "Go on, you wicked beast," she said. Pajti was not giving up his prize. Baring his fangs, he let out a low growl. He advanced slowly on her, ready to spring. This was too much even for Cook. She ran from the kitchen, shouting for help. Pajti wolfed down the cake.

As soon as she was gone, the boy darted into the kitchen. "Good boy," he said to Pajti, but Pajti turned on the boy and growled at him. The boy knocked two more cakes on the floor for Pajti. The dog fell on them while the boy grabbed one cake for himself and fled.

He ran across the back court and shoved cake into his mouth. He must not be caught with it. Behind one of the hydrangeas in the outer courtyard, he had pruned a hiding spot where he could nap away the hottest hours of the afternoon. If he could just make it there, he could take his time with the rest of the cake.

He slid around the corner to the outer courtyard only to find his master, Casimir, talking to the Factor. Behind them stood Rodrigo, one of the more senior slaves and valet to Casimir's son Tibor. The boy saw them just before they noticed him. He jammed the rest of the cake into his mouth and dropped to his hands and knees. As the three of them looked over at him, he pressed his forehead to the ground. Abasing himself gave him just enough time to give the cake a quick chew before swallowing it.

"What about that one? Surely we don't need him," said Casimir.

The boy stood. Slaves had to keep their heads bowed in Casimir's presence, but the boy made sure not to bow his head too far. Dealing directly with Casimir was dangerous. It was always a good idea to keep an eye on the master.

Casimir looked down at the boy. When his eye landed on the ring hanging around the boy's neck, he twisted his great waxed mustache as if he were trying to remember something. "What's your name again?"

"I haven't got one, Master," said the boy.

"Why not? Did you lose it?" Casimir laughed out loud. "That's a good one, isn't it?" he said to the Factor. "Did you lose it?"

The Factor managed to produce a dry chuckle. "Yes, sir, very droll indeed," he said.

"Oh no, Master, if someone gave me something as valuable as a name, I would never lose it," said the boy.

"You cheeky little devil!" shouted Casimir. He clouted the boy on the ear. "You think you need a tongue to, to— What is it you do around here?"

"I tend the plants in the inner and outer courtyards, Master," said the boy.

"That's it?" said Casimir. "For that, I give you two meals every day?" He shook his head. "You're going to Mossglum."

"Why?" said the boy.

Rodrigo gasped.

The Factor stared, wide-eyed.

But Casimir remained calm. "Did you just ask me why?"

"Uh—"

"First my son wants to know why, and now my slave does," said Casimir. "I suppose unquestioning obedience is terribly old-fashioned nowadays." He pursed his lips. "I suppose I must be an old fuddy-duddy for expecting it."

"The young do have their notions," said the Factor.

"You want to know why?" said Casimir. "Here's why." The blow staggered the boy. His ears rang, and he had to blink his eyes for several seconds to clear his vision. "But since you asked, I am sending my eldest son, Tibor"—at the mention of Tibor's name, the Factor rolled his eyes—"to the town of Mossglum to, to, to . . ." Casimir turned to the Factor. "Hang me, what is he going to do there again?"

"I believe you are sending him to the home of your wife's cousin so that he may better understand the industry that converts manure to fertilizer," said the Factor.

"That's it," said Casimir. "He's going to Mossglum to learn about dung."

"A very exciting opportunity for a young man to make his mark in the world, I'm sure," said the Factor.

"I was going to send him with Rodrigo, but that's not good enough, apparently. He can't make do with just one slave. And since all you do is slop a bit of water about, I thought I'd send you, too," said Casimir. "Is that a good enough reason? Does that satisfy your curiosity?"

The boy opened his mouth, but before he could say anything, Casimir shoved the boy at Rodrigo. Rodrigo caught the boy's shoulder and led him away.

"You have the luck of the Foul One," said Rodrigo as they climbed the back stair. "Why he didn't have the skin whipped from your back, I don't know."

"Won't they need my back to carry things?" said the boy.

♠

Duke Geoffrey was a well-educated man. He could even read on his own. It was not something he did very often. He preferred to nod wisely and say, "Yes, I see," while one of his scribes read aloud to him. For this book, however, he made an exception. By decree of the College of Wizards, owning an unsanctioned spell book was punishable by death. Duke Geoffrey would have to silence any man who knew of the book's existence, and scribes were expensive to replace.

He read from the old book with great care. He moved

his lips with each word and sounded out the particularly hard ones to make sure he had them right.

But his efforts went unrewarded. The spell book had come to him from his great-aunt, a leading witch of her day. As Duke Geoffrey fought his way down the table of contents, he began to wonder if she had not been a little mad, too. Why else would she bother to write down something as useless as "A Spell for Summoning a Crane," page 67? This gem was followed by "A Spell for Summoning a Crow," page 89. In turn, there were spells for calling forth a deer, a donkey and then a dormouse.

It infuriated Duke Geoffrey. His situation was desperate. The King was plotting to cheat him of his rightful place in the line of succession. The King was maneuvering to have his daughter, Princess Alice—*a girl*—inherit the throne. It was all so grossly unfair.

Someone had to stop this calamity, and Duke Geoffrey knew he was someone. He also knew better than to risk everything by sending his knights and men-at-arms to attack the capital. He could gain the throne without starting an all-out war if he could just find the right spell. But he would need something more powerful than this heap of parlor tricks.

"Dormouse" was followed by "Doukhobor" and then "duck." Duke Geoffrey stopped. He had never heard of a Doukhobor, but it sounded Eastern. And unpleasant. Perhaps it was a mountain beast or bog creature. Duke Geoffrey turned to page 174. It took him six pages and an hour to learn that a Doukhobor was an obscure type of peasant who refused to wear clothes.

Duke Geoffrey swept the spell book from the table. He had already upped the rents twice this year. He did not need *more* naked peasants. The fire, that was the place for this useless thing. When he picked it up to fling it there, he froze. There, on page 180, was "A Spell for Summoning a Dragon." Duke Geoffrey flipped back to the table of contents. It went from "Doukhobor," page 174, to "duck," page 196. There was no mention of "dragon." He smiled. That witch had hidden the gold in the pig slop, cunning old girl. Duke Geoffrey didn't even bother to search the book for more treasures. He turned back to page 180 and studied the spell carefully. The ingredients would be expensive, and the rituals complicated, but—a dragon! Duke Geoffrey's eyes glittered as he saw himself issuing orders to a dragon. A *dragon.*

The boy's back was needed to carry things. Many things. In addition to many fine suits of clothes, Tibor planned to bring a few books of poetry, to pass the time, and several boxes of jewelry, to dress up his suits. He also needed a dozen decks of cards, for entertaining other young gentlemen. And when the company was mixed, he would require a quantity of gaming boards, because proper ladies never touched cards. Then there were several decorative wall hangings, as his quarters were sure to be dreary. And a comfortable chair. Also an additional, slightly less comfortable though still quite serviceable, chair. And a small writing desk. And so on.

This was all on top of the food, blankets and other traveling gear necessary for such a trip. In the end, the pile of luggage exceeded even Casimir's optimistic view of what two slaves could sanely be called upon to carry, which led to a huge argument.

Tibor's opinion was that as he was the eldest son of the richest and most important merchant in all of High Albemarle, he needed to make a proper impression on the people of Mossglum. This could only be done by an ostentatious display of wealth.

Casimir's view was that Mossglum was a bit out of the way, and the people would be impressed by any display of finery, even one much less than Tibor was proposing.

Tibor responded that Mossglum was indeed a no-where little backwater, if not a boggy hole, and Casimir was sending Tibor there at the beginning of the marriage season because Casimir hated Tibor, even though Tibor was his most dutiful and respectful son.

Casimir countered that Tibor was a churlish wastrel who ought to be grateful that he had not long since been sold to the silver mines in light of his various misdeeds, which Casimir proceeded to enumerate at length and in detail.

And so it went.

Rodrigo and the boy spent the argument alternately packing and unpacking the bags, adding and removing various items as the argument shifted first in Tibor's favor and then in Casimir's. After many, many hours of shouts, curses, accusations and tears, Tibor settled for riding his second-best horse and bringing only twenty-seven suits of clothes. Rodrigo used his familiarity with Tibor's wardrobe to arrange it so that most of the heavier items wound up in the boy's pack. Though it must be said, both strained mightily under the amount of luggage Casimir finally authorized. Obviously, Tibor's horse carried nothing other than Tibor, and Tibor himself carried nothing at all.

A mile's walk from Casimir's villa was the Great Eastern Way, the broad road that ran from Albemarle City, the capital of High Albemarle, to Mossglum and on to lands farther east. Albemarle City was supposed to be beautiful. So beautiful, it was said, that the High King, who ruled nearly the whole of the world, preferred it to any other city in his domain, even his own capital.

When Tibor, Rodrigo and the boy came to the Way, Tibor pointed west toward Albemarle City. "That's where I should be going. The marriage season starts in a week," he said. Tibor was a few years older than the boy and of proper age to seek a match. Tibor looked toward Albemarle City for so long, the boy began to worry that he might actually go there, but Tibor was as obedient as any of Casimir's slaves. They turned their backs on Albemarle City and headed east.

At first, the Great Eastern Way was bounded by grand estates and sprawling tea plantations. As the road led away from the sea, the land grew drier, and the great plantations dwindled down to miserable dirt farms. By the third day, there was nothing but dry prairie covered in head-high wild grasses. No matter what kind of lands they traveled through, Tibor sulked. For his part, Rodrigo set his jaw and stared at the horizon. So the boy trudged along in silence.

When they stopped for lunch on the third day, Tibor came alive for the first time. "It's not fair," he complained to his slaves between bites of his third sausage. "Why did Father send me away?"

Rodrigo silently munched on his hunk of cheese. The boy nibbled on a piece of dry bread.

"I'll tell you why," said Tibor. "It's because he prefers Milan to me." Milan was Casimir's second-eldest son. "Have I done anything to deserve such treatment?"

It took a long moment for the boy to realize that Tibor expected one of them to answer this question. "Nothing, Master," he said.

"Even a slave can see it," said Tibor. "What kind of way is that for a father to treat a son? How did your father treat you?"

"I didn't know him," said the boy. "Nor my mam."

Tibor nodded. Turning to Rodrigo, he said, "But you knew your father, yes?"

Rodrigo took a long, slow look at Tibor. "He died when I was nine," he said. "When our village was overrun."

"But how did he treat you before then?" said Tibor.

"My father was a good man," said Rodrigo. "He loved his family and died trying to save us." His eyes grew moist.

"You see," said Tibor. "He loved you and wanted the best for you. He spent time with you and taught you things. He gave up everything for you, just as a father should, right?"

Rodrigo was not going to answer, so the boy said, "Yes, Master."

"Exactly," said Tibor. He patted Rodrigo on the shoulder. "It's why we had to sell Erzsebet. You'd have wanted to spend time with her and the baby. It's only natural." A few weeks earlier, Erzsebet and her newborn daughter had been sold. The boy had not known that Rodrigo was the father. "It was a hard choice for me, but in the long run, it was for the best. I think we can both see that now. This way, we can both get back to concentrating on my career and marriage prospects."

Rodrigo nodded. He stood and walked to the edge of the road. But he did not relieve himself. Instead, he picked up a rock the size of a melon and brought it back with him. The boy was puzzled by this, and couldn't see why Rodrigo would come to a stop directly behind Tibor.

"Rodrigo, what are you doing?" said Tibor, but he did not turn to look back at his slave.

As soon as Rodrigo raised the rock over Tibor's head, the boy knew what Rodrigo was about to do. He squeezed his eyes shut so he would not have to see what came next. He covered his ears with his hands and sat in silent darkness for what seemed like a long time. When he could take it no longer, he opened one eye and peeked at the scene in front of him.

Tibor lay on his side in the dirt. His one exposed eye was open. It pointed slackly down at the ground. He did not move at all; even his chest did not rise or fall. The boy had never seen anyone lie so perfectly still before. Rodrigo's rock sat a little way behind Tibor. Strangely, there were only a few spatters of blood on it.

The boy opened his other eye and uncovered his ears. He looked up at Rodrigo. It was said that the Foul One sometimes took hold of a slave and made him attack his master. But the boy could see no sign of the Foul One in Rodrigo's eyes. He just looked a little tired.

For his part, Rodrigo studied Tibor's body. "That was a hard choice for me," said Rodrigo. A little smile crept onto his lips. "But in the long run, it was for the best. I think we can both see that now."

The boy realized he was the only witness to Rodrigo's

terrible crime. Slowly, he began to creep away, but this only drew Rodrigo's attention. Rodrigo looked over at the boy, as if he had only just remembered the boy was there. "Please, I . . . ," said the boy, but he did not know how to finish. He had never tried to convince someone not to murder him before.

Rodrigo stepped over Tibor's body and went back to his bread and cheese. "You've nothing to fear," he said. "I've no quarrel with you."

"Is he . . . is he dead?" said the boy. He really ought to go over to Tibor and see if he could do anything for him. But he could not bring himself to go any closer.

"Should be," said Rodrigo through his lunch. He stopped chewing and glanced over at Tibor. "Or do you think he needs another crack?"

"No!" said the boy. It was all so strange, so unnatural, that the boy did not know what to say. Finally, he spluttered, "How could you? He . . . he is your master."

"Was," Rodrigo corrected.

"But the law—you know what they do," said the boy. A slave who raised his hand against his master was tortured and burned alive.

"They have to catch me first," said Rodrigo, standing up.

The boy watched as Rodrigo dragged Tibor's body deep into the tall grasses so it could not be seen. He took Tibor's coin purse and dressed in one of Tibor's suits before untethering Tibor's horse. Holding the horse's reins, he turned to the boy and said, "She'll carry two as easily as one."

The boy gasped. Running away would mean defying the fate the gods had picked for him. Of course, Rodrigo had already defied the will of the gods when he killed his master. Still, the boy was not going to follow in his footsteps. "Oh, no, no," said the boy. "I'll go back to the master's estate, if it's all the same to you."

"You know he'll burn you for helping me," said Rodrigo.

"But I didn't help you," said the boy. "He'll believe me when I tell him." He tried to picture that actually happening.

"Then he'll burn you for failing to do your utmost for your master," said Rodrigo.

That made the boy queasy. Slaves were supposed to give up their lives to protect their masters. It was the Fifth of the Ninety-Nine Duties of a Slave. He had done nothing to save Tibor. Rodrigo probably would have killed him if he had tried. But then, at least, he would have gone to the gods with a pure soul.

When the boy had no answer, Rodrigo said, "Maybe you'd have been content to droil away all your days for that fiend and his father. Doesn't seem like much of a life to me, but I did take it from you without your leave. And for that, I'm sorry." He mounted the horse. "I wish you luck, boy. You'll need it." He turned the horse to ride away.

"Have you no fear of the Pit?" said the boy. Those who defied the will of the gods were cast into the Pit of Eternal Torment, slaves of the Foul One for all eternity.

Rodrigo glanced back. "None," he said. "For if this is truly the life the gods want for us, we're already there." He turned away again, and this time, he rode off.

2

Plain Alice stalked across the barnyard, milking bucket in hand, the corners of her mouth turned down in an almighty scowl. The list of those invited to the next agon was out. And for the third time, her name was not on it. It was ridiculous. Even Young Hubert was on the list, and everyone knew his head was better suited for driving nails than cracking books. Of course, his father's favorite aunt was married to the brother of the secretary of the Council of Sages, so it was probably just a courtesy invitation. Surely no one thought he had a chance of winning an ordinary. But Plain Alice could. Or she could if the

Council would give her the chance to compete instead of wasting invitations on thickwit boys like Hubert. Instead, she was stuck milking Old Bess.

The unfairness of Plain Alice's life so consumed her mind that she never saw the great shadow racing across the ground, overtaking her. One moment, she was stomping toward the barn. The next, she was jerked up into the air, her legs dancing in the nothingness. She screamed, as that seemed like the natural thing to do. But she was a practical girl, so when nothing came of screaming, she gave it up in favor of making a study of her situation. The claws of some tremendous beast grasped her firmly by the shoulders and snagged in her long red hair. She looked up at its scaly underbelly. To each side of her were great bat wings pounding away at the air, pulling the two of them into the sky. Behind them trailed a long thin tail that ended in a spade tip. The dragon, for that was what the creature had to be, lifted her higher and higher into the sky.

She battered at the dragon's mighty claws with the milking bucket and screamed, "Let me go! Let me go!" until she thought better of it. At this height, if the dragon let go, she would plunge to her doom. Still, presence of mind can be hard to come by when one is being kidnapped by a monster. For his part, the dragon ignored her.

After a few minutes of climbing, the dragon leveled off and wheeled to the east. Over her shoulder, Plain

Alice watched Middlebury roll away until even the towers of the Earl's keep could no longer be seen. The dragon flew fast, far faster than a horse at full gallop. Soon she could make out the black walls and towers of Castle Geoffrey, even though it lay nearly a day's march to the east of Middlebury. The imposing castle served as the seat of Duke Geoffrey, the King's cousin and potential heir to the throne. People liked to say that Duke Geoffrey was the only man in West Stanhope ambitious enough to want it, rich enough to build it and vain enough to name it after himself. As they passed over it, the Duke's men scrambled about in a panic. An optimistic few loosed arrows at them, but they were far too high in the air.

Castle Geoffrey receded as quickly as it had arrived. Beyond it were moors and eventually the Little Dismal. Despite its name, the Little Dismal was a vast swampy forest of cypress trees and hanging mosses. It was called little only because the Great Dismal, just over the Mountains of Fire in East Stanhope, was even bigger. But they did not fly over the Great Dismal, for when they reached the Mountains of Fire, the dragon turned north. Soon enough, they came to a place of strange rock formations. There was a series of natural columns of basalt that rose into the air.

The dragon set Plain Alice on the tallest of these columns and then landed on the ground. Plain Alice looked around quickly. It was thirty feet down to the ground, and the nearest column was fifteen feet away. "There's no way I can get down from here," she said, mostly to herself.

To her surprise, the dragon responded, "Well, why do you think I put you there?" She had not known that dragons could talk.

♠

Every man has a fate. Before he is born, the Three Sisters draw a lot from the great stone bowl to see what that fate will be. King or commoner, soldier or scholar, notable or merchant, everyone has a fate, and it is their duty to submit graciously to that fate. It is the will of the gods. When the boy was born, the Three Sisters had drawn slave as his fatestone, so it was only just, decent and proper that he be a good slave.

And the boy did try. A good slave thanked the gods for his fate. Every morning, the boy went down on all fours, pressed his forehead to the ground seven times and thanked the Three Sisters for making him a slave. And when he was done, he pressed his forehead to the ground another time and asked the Chained Man, the god of the slaves, to help him be a better slave. This was the First Duty of a Slave. A good slave never raised his hand to his master. That was the Fourth Duty, and the boy never had. The boy had sometimes—not often, but once in a while—even loved his master. At least, he thought that it might be love. It was hard to be sure. Still, it ought to count for something because everyone said the Third Duty was the hardest. All of that, the boy got right.

The trouble was, it took more than that to be a good slave. A good slave obeyed his master in all things. That was the Second Duty. A good slave did not filch food, which violated the Tenth Duty. And he did not smart-mouth his master, which violated the Eleventh Duty. Or maybe the Twelfth. There were ninety-nine, so it was easy to muddle them up. And a good slave absolutely did not waste whole afternoons hiding behind hydrangea bushes, imagining he was a hero from The Tales—a falsely enslaved prince who had to battle three monsters, each more terrible than the last, before being restored to titles, lands and a palace full of slaves of his own. There was no Duty covering that specifically, but it definitely violated several of them.

A good slave would have died trying to protect Tibor from harm. That was the Fifth Duty. And a good slave would not run away—Sixth Duty—even if going back to Tibor's villa meant being burned at the stake.

Being a good slave was not easy, obviously. Still, that was the will of the gods. Deep down, the boy really did *want* to be good. There had even been days when he *was* good. Just not this day.

Wicked as it was, the boy chose not to be burned alive. He was defying the will of the gods. He was a renegade, just like Rodrigo. And like Rodrigo, he would serve the Foul One in the Pit in the next life.

At least he had the decency to feel bad about it, unlike Rodrigo. And that counted for something. Or he hoped it did.

He went through Tibor's bags, looking for something to wear. Heading on to Mossglum seemed like a bad idea. Rodrigo went that way. Also, Tibor was expected there and would soon be missed. Since he could not go back the way he came, that left bushwhacking through the grasslands. For that, he needed more than the simple cotton breechcloth he always wore.

While he pawed through Tibor's suits, he tried to reassure himself that he was not really running away. He was only trying to avoid being burned. Once he could prove that he had not caused Tibor's death, he would go back and be a slave, as he was supposed to.

Besides, if he burned, Casimir would lose a slave. He might not fetch as high a price as a horse or a good hunting dog, but he was still worth *something.* So if the boy could somehow prove his innocence, he would save Casimir a needless loss. And protecting his master's property was the Eighth Duty.

Of course, there was also the matter of Casimir's rights as a property owner. The boy's life belonged to Casimir, and the boy was not supposed to concern himself with what Casimir chose to do with it. That was the Seventh Duty. It was all very complicated.

He found himself worrying the ring he wore about

his neck. He often did when thinking over a knotty problem. He stopped, laid it flat on his hand and looked at it. It was plain and heavy and looked to be made of iron. He always thought of it as his father's ring, though he knew almost nothing of his father or his mother. At some point, someone had mentioned that the ring had something to do with his father, but the boy could never remember who had told him this. Somewhere along the way, someone had tried to destroy it. It had been smashed over and over again with a hammer, leaving it cracked open and misshapen. His father must have been a very large man, as the ring was much wider around than most. The boy gave it one more rub before going back to Tibor's baggage.

In the end, he settled on a green woolen hunting suit, which was sturdy and warm. The leather riding suit probably would have been better, but Tibor was still wearing it. The boy could not even look at Tibor, much less touch him. So the boy put on the hunting suit instead, cinching the belt way down and rolling the arms and legs up to get it to fit. The suit felt strange; he had never worn trousers or a shirt before.

Stepping into the tall grasses was like being plunged into another world. The grass grew so thick the boy had to use his arms to pull open a path to walk along. It rose over his head, blocking his view of everything but a small patch of sky. The boy's whole world shrank down to just a few feet around him. The going was hard but helped him keep his thoughts from the enormity of his crimes.

By nightfall, he was worn out. His arms and back were sore from struggling through the tangle of grass. He ate the little food he had. He meant to save some, but it was gone before he knew it. Exhausted, he threw himself down onto a little nest of grass and dreamed of Tibor with his dead eye pointed slackly at the ground.

The boy woke early, went down on all fours, pressed his forehead to the ground seven times and then stopped. He felt a clutch at his heart. He could hardly give thanks to the Three Sisters for making him a slave. Nor could he pray to the Chained Man. The Chained Man wanted him to go back to Casimir's and be burned. He could almost see the Chained Man raging and cursing at him. It was enough to get him up and walking.

After four days, the grasslands, which had seemed as though they might go on forever, suddenly came to an end in a low range of gray and stony foothills. The hills themselves were mostly free of greenery, though a few scrubby trees halfheartedly tried to grow in the gullies between them. Beyond the hills rose an immense range of mountains.

The boy knew The Tales by heart. He had eavesdropped on the telling of every one at least a dozen times. Of all of them, the hardest to believe was The Tale of the

Seven Silent Gentlemen. In that one, the cooper's daughter escaped the seven silent gentlemen by jumping from the top of the highest peak in the land to the moon when it passed by. She rode the moon across the sky to safety while the seven silent gentlemen fell to their deaths trying to jump after her. The boy had never believed that Tale, not until he saw those mountains. They started with a wall of snowcapped black peaks rising up into the sky. Behind them lay another line of mountains and then another and another, each soaring higher and still higher than the last, until they were just white peaks floating on top of the clouds.

This had to be the Spine, the great mountain range that ran the length of the Kingdoms. People traveled to the lands north of the Spine, or so the boy had heard. But he could see no way across. So he turned and followed the foothills instead.

After half a day, he came to a narrow rut of a road that was little more than a trail. In one direction, it twisted into the foothills of the Spine, slowly rising. In the other, it ran out across the grasslands, where the boy saw a mule train slowly heading his way. Although it would be safer to avoid other people, his belly would not let him. He had not eaten in days. When there had been no prospect of food, his stomach had only troubled him a little. Now that there was a chance, his stomach demanded food. So he sat on the side of the road to see if he could cadge a little bread from them.

♠

Plain Alice's father, Oswald the Sage, happened to be watching when the dragon stole her away. He had spent that morning sitting at his desk, stroking his beard and shuffling his receipts about in the hopes that in so doing, somehow, some part of his debts could be made to disappear. It did not work. No matter how many different ways he added it up, the dispiritingly long column of figures always came to just shy of forty silver sovereigns, as much as his farm was worth. It was a debt that he would never be able to repay.

On the other side of the window, Plain Alice stormed her way to the barn. Seeing her should have brought him a few minutes' peace of mind, but her anger only reminded him of another of his failures: he could not get her invited to an agon. He should have had an in. He was a sage himself, after all. And he saw other men do it. At the meetings, they thumped each other on the back and told a few jokes. Then someone would whisper something in someone else's ear—the right someone else—and a little while later, the Council would vote for it. Somehow, though, he had never worked out which backs to thump, or what jokes to tell, or whose ear to whisper what into. So the Council never invited her, which meant that she could never win an ordinary, which meant that she could never apprentice to become a sage, which was what she wanted more than anything else in the world. All because

Oswald had failed her. He was, he thought, as miserable as a man could be.

Then the dragon carried Plain Alice away.

At once, Oswald jumped up and ran for the back door. On his way through the kitchen, he grabbed the first thing that came to hand: an old iron soup ladle. He ran out into the yard, waved his ladle as menacingly as he could and screamed for the dragon to bring Plain Alice back. The dragon took no notice. He kept a firm grip on Plain Alice and beat his great leathery wings. Higher and higher he rose, paying no attention to the small, stoop-shouldered man, jumping up and down, waving a spoon and weeping bitterly.

After a moment, Oswald gave up jumping and shouting. He tried to think what to do. Thinking was the only thing Oswald was good at. It was the reason he'd become a sage. But he could not bring his mind to focus. Seemingly of its own will, it flooded with terrible images of all the dreadful things the dragon might do to Alice.

Part of the problem was that no one knew very much about dragons. The texts were clear that dragons liked to carry off young maidens, but no one had the least idea *why.* All anyone knew was that it took at least a knight, if not a lord, to rescue a young maiden from a dragon, and Oswald had no way to attract a knight to his cause. The usual reward for such a rescue was the young maiden's hand in marriage, but Alice would flay him if he tried to marry her off to some knight. Anyway, knights wanted to marry princesses. Oh, a knight might settle for the daughter of an earl, but the daughter of a penniless sage and the heirship of a bankrupt farm would not be much of a draw. A reward of gold would do, of course, but Oswald did not have any. There was only one course left to him.

Oswald dressed in his least patched suit and combed his long beard. Then he put on the wig he inherited from a great-uncle who had done well in the costermongery. The wig was only a little one, barely big enough to cover his bald spot, and it had not been powdered in decades. Still, it was the best he had, so he wore it.

He set out through town toward the Earl's keep. Many people had seen Plain Alice's abduction, and the news had spread. As Oswald walked through town, all manner of people asked him, "Is it true?" Or, "Can it be so?" Or, worst of all, "What're you going to do?" To each, Oswald simply said, "I'm off to see the Earl." Then, because all of the townsfolk were fond of both Oswald and Alice, and because seeing the Earl was the only thing anyone could do, and because, quite frankly, Alice's kidnapping was the most exciting thing to happen in Middlebury since a troll had run amok fourteen years earlier, each of them joined Oswald. Along came Elvin the Blacksmith, Arnold the Baker, Dervla the Milkmaid, Jonathan the Clerk, and dozens and dozens more, until half the town had an excuse to dodge that day's work.

♠

The boy sat on the side of the road as mule after mule, each saddled with two strongboxes, shuffled by. Most of the mule drivers ignored the boy and concentrated on their work. One, however, broke away from a spot near the end of the train and came to speak to the boy. Even though he wore a friendly expression, his face had hard lines on it. "Afternoon, son. I'm Nikola." From the bottom of his chin hung a long, narrow beard with beads braided into it. "What's your name?"

"I haven't got one," said the boy.

Nikola nodded and tapped his nose. "Understood, understood. Best to keep these things to yourself when you're on the road," he said, and put his hand out.

Duty pulled at the boy's forehead, tugging it toward the ground, but the boy caught himself just in time. Only slaves abased themselves; free men shook hands. The boy stuck his hand out, but when Nikola took it, the boy's thumb wound up stuck between their palms. The boy knew at once that he had done it wrong. He had to do better next time if he was to avoid being found out.

For his part, Nikola didn't seem to notice. "Still, on the prowl for an adventure, if I am any judge. And I am. I am. Ain't I, young man?" he said without releasing the boy's hand.

Not only had he never shaken a man's hand, he had never been called a young man before. He was old enough that some might have called him a young man, at least sometimes, had he been free. But slaves were always boys, even when they were old and gray. "Uh, I guess so," said the boy.

"Knew it. Knew it. Knew it to be so," said Nikola, still not releasing the boy's hand. "We're headed up to the mines at Mount Dragoman to pick up a load of silver. Then it's back to Albemarle City. You're welcome to join us and see where we take you." Something about the way he said it struck the boy as odd.

"I don't have any money," said the boy, trying to free his hand and take a step back.

Nikola clapped his other hand on the boy's shoulder and gripped it firmly. "No need to worry on that, son. It's not such a long trip. You can pay your way with your company," said Nikola. He raised his voice a bit. "We're all pretty heartily sick of one another by now, ain't we, boys?"

The men just grumbled and shrugged.

"That's very kind, sir. Thank you," said the boy. Nikola seemed to be friendly enough, but his hunger for the boy to join the caravan was strange. "It wouldn't feel right taking advantage of your kindness like that. Maybe if you could just spare a little bread?"

Nikola still did not let him go. "Are you sure? I'd hate for a hungry lad to miss our rabbit stew," he said. "Almost as much as I'd hate to have him offend my hospitality."

"Rabbit stew?" said the boy. He shivered a little in hunger.

"Rich and savory and plenty of it," said Nikola.

Perhaps he had misjudged Nikola. He *was* a little odd, but some men are just odd. He was probably harmless. And there was rabbit stew. "I'd hate to offend your hospitality," said the boy.

"Then it's signed and sealed. Done, done, done and done," said Nikola. He put his arm over the boy's shoulder and hustled him along to catch up with the mule train. "Stout lad like you reminds me of a son of my own."

"You've a son my age?" asked the boy.

"Oh, probably. Who knows?" said Nikola. He scanned the caravan for his spot. When he found it, he escorted the boy to it. Only then did he release the boy. "I'm the caravan master," he said, though the boy had not asked. "I have to be able to see what's going on all along the caravan." Nikola swept his arm to take in the length of the caravan, but his eye never left the nearest strongbox.

For the rest of the day, Nikola regaled the boy with a seemingly endless chain of tales of his romantic misadventures with the various ladies of Albemarle City. The ladies in these stories nearly always turned out to be married, though never to Nikola. The boy was shocked by the casual way Nikola bragged about his scandalous behavior, but said nothing for fear of offending his new host. He also noticed that even when Nikola acted out his outrageous escapes from vengeful husbands, he never strayed far from his strongbox.

♠

As Oswald's procession advanced on the keep, Godric, Earl of Middlebury, watched from a parapet with mounting dread. The watch had already reported the kidnapping. The Earl knew what would come next. He was about to be humiliated, and there was nothing he could do about it. The Earl straightened his wig and went down to his main hall to receive the petitioning party. The townsfolk poured into the great hall until it was fuller than the Earl had seen it in many years. He wanted to get this over with, but there were traditions to be upheld. So he waited until the crowd thrust Oswald forward. Oswald bowed a little and, with great formality, said, "My Lord of Middlebury—"

The Earl rose from his chair and took Oswald's hand in his own. The crowd fell silent. This was not the sort of thing that earls did. "Oswald the Sage, my old friend," said the Earl. And they were old friends, after a fashion. Back when Oswald was the most promising boy in Middlebury, the Earl had sponsored Oswald's apprenticeship as part of his plan to build Middlebury up into a proper market town. He had been a young and ambitious earl once. "I know why you are here. I know of your pain—"

"Then you must do something," said Oswald, not even realizing he had dared to interrupt the Earl.

"I cannot," said the Earl. "What few hairs I have left are white." The Earl judged himself no longer in fit condition to quest after monsters. It was not so much that he feared meeting the dragon on the field of honor. If the worst happened, he would at least be spared the nuisance of being the Earl of Middlebury anymore. No, he simply could not stomach the journey. Just the thought of dragging his aching old bones back and forth across the countryside and camping in the mud for weeks on end gave him a headache.

"My son is crippled," said the Earl. Lord Arthur, the Earl's son, had never fully recovered from the injuries he received slaying a troll fourteen years back. The Honorable Aidan, the Earl's grandson, bravely offered to go, obliging the Earl to explain that six-year-olds were not allowed to fight dragons, which led to a howling temper tantrum.

"I have no knights." Usually the Earl had several knights clotting up his castle, mostly his ne'er-do-well nephews. But lately, knights were in mysteriously short supply all over West Stanhope. Of course, knights mostly got into brawls in taverns or chased after shopkeepers' daughters, so the Earl counted their disappearance a blessing. At least, he did until he needed a few.

"My counting house is empty." The same poor harvest that threatened to bankrupt Oswald had resulted in short rents and missed tax payments for the Earl as well. He simply did not have ready money for rewards.

"I must reject your petition," said the Earl. The crowd was silent.

"But what am I to do?" wailed Oswald, sounding

more like a lost child than a scholar. "Am I to chase down the dragon with my pitchfork?"

"No," said the Earl. "You will travel to Farnham. There, you will petition the King himself to come to our aid." The crowd gasped. A few of them had been to Farnham at one time or another. One or two had even seen the King in procession. But no one had ever spoken to the King, much less petitioned him for anything.

Oswald was so lost in his own worry and grief that he failed to recognize the solemnity of his charge. "But will he help?" asked Oswald.

"The King is not just our ruler. He is our protector. He must help," the Earl assured him. "You must go at once."

3

King Julian II, Monarch of West Stanhope and Lord of All Its Assorted Dependencies, held his ear to the conservatory door and strained to hear. If pressed, the King would have been forced to admit that eavesdropping on his daughter, Princess Alice, and her latest gaggle of friends was likely beneath the dignity of so august a personage as himself. But there was nothing else he could do. The King was a desperate man.

On the far side of the door, a girl said, "Hmm . . . hmm . . . I'm not sure." It was that Dulcinea girl from Pfeppenwald. Or was it Graffenthorpe. Somewhere like that. It didn't really matter where she came from, as long as she could be sent back there. "Lord Harcourt of Hinchlow?" she said.

A chorus of girls' voices cried out, "Oooh!" followed by a lot of giggling. The King sighed. There was always giggling, and he could never figure out what they were giggling about.

"Alfred the Younger," said another girl, one whose voice the King did not recognize.

This suggestion was met with silence.

"He's Sir Osric's squire," said the girl. "His ears stick out a bit." There was still no response. The King could almost hear the others avoiding her eyes, poor girl.

"What about you, Your Highness, what do you think?" said a third girl. She was either Lady Beatrice or the Honorable Serena, Lord Sydenham's youngest. The King was not sure which.

"The most handsome man at court?" said the Princess. "I'd say Sir Keevan."

The King stiffened. Sir Keevan was a fop and a twit. For their part, the girls all collapsed into giggles again.

"What about that purple cravat he always wears?" said Dulcinea.

"I think it's rather dashing," said the Princess. "Besides, I hear that purple is all the rage in the Imperial City." So she was getting fashion reports from the High King's court, too. The gods alone knew how she was managing that.

There was nothing for it. He had to get rid of them all, including Dulcinea and Lady Beatrice—or was it the Honorable Serena? He would send them both away, just to be safe. Nor could Sir Keevan be allowed to distract the Princess. He would have to go as well, though that was trickier. He could not just be packed off teary-eyed to his father's country estate. Of course, an inspection tour of the kingdom's defenses would keep him away for a month or two. And a good jawboning from the Chamberlain would probably be enough to convince him that it was some great honor. He really was that thick.

"Julie! What are you doing?"

King Julian jumped away from the door and spun around to face Queen Ludmilla. "Nothing," he said, a little too quickly. Then he added, "Dear." That did not seem to help.

The Queen fixed him with a suspicious stare. She pressed her own ear to the door for a moment. "Julie," she said, a note of accusation creeping into her voice. "Eavesdropping on our daughter?"

"But you don't understand," he said. "It's all clothes and boys and . . . and giggling." The giggling really was the worst part. "She's becoming frivolous."

"She's just at that age," said the Queen.

That was the trouble with daughters. They were always at one age or another. "If she's to become a monarch, she must learn to conduct herself with the seriousness of a monarch."

The Queen raised a single eyebrow at him. "Perhaps you could teach her how to conduct herself like a monarch by showing her how to sneak down back halls and listen in on other people's conversations."

Long ago, the King had set himself the goal of winning an argument with his wife. Once again, that day had failed to arrive. Fortunately, at just that moment one of his daughter's tutors came around the corner. The tutor was a short, bald man who was constantly perspiring. When he saw the King and Queen, his forehead immediately went damp. He turned bright red and bowed deeply. "I do beg your pardon, Your Majesties," he said. "I—"

"Shouldn't you be giving the Princess her lessons?" said the King. He might not be able to win against the Queen, but he could distract her.

"Yes, Your Majesty," said the tutor. "But—"

"She gave you the slip," said the Queen. "Again."

"Well—"

"She's in there," said the Queen, pointing to the conservatory.

"Gossiping," added the King. The look the Queen gave him was enough to tell him he had not gotten himself off the hook yet.

"Thank you, Your Majesty," said the tutor. He contrived to make himself thin enough to slide between the King and the door without touching either one.

The King had no intention of letting him get away, not

while the Queen was still annoyed at him. He dropped his hand on the tutor's shoulder heavily enough to make the man squeal. "And what lesson should she be having now?" he said. Whatever the answer was, it was sure to displease the Queen.

"Elocution, Your Majesty," said the tutor. "To be followed by ballroom dancing."

The Queen visited a mighty scowl on the man. "I will have no more of such nonsense," she said. "From now on, it shall be nothing but history."

The tutor turned to the King for help. "Your Majesty, with all due respect, history is hardly a fit subject for young ladies," he said. Tutors were hired by the Chamberlain, and the Chamberlain's ideas about the proper education for a princess ran to needlework and curtseying.

"As always, my wife speaks for me," said the King. "We will need a new lesson plan. I will instruct the Chamberlain to draw one up."

"Again," said the Queen in irritation. New lessons plans were drawn up frequently, but the actual lessons never seemed to change.

"But starting now, the Princess will learn history," said the King. "And law."

"And mathematics," added the Queen.

"Mathematics?" gasped the tutor. A new round of sweat broke out on his forehead.

"If the Princess is to take up my crown when I am

gone—and I think we would both prefer that to the other possibility . . ." The tutor turned pale, and the King could hardly blame him. The prospect of Duke Geoffrey on the throne was enough to make even the hardiest man go pale. "If she is to rule, she must be prepared." The King leaned in so close their noses almost touched. "I will not have her become frivolous." The King stood up straight and released the tutor.

"Now see to it," said the Queen.

"Yes, Your Majesties. At once, Your Majesties," said the tutor, and he slipped away through the door to the conservatory.

♠

". . . and when that old carpenter hears me screaming for water, he thinks the floodwaters have come sure. He cuts his rope, and his tub comes crashing to the floor with a thunder like you wouldn't believe. The old fool even breaks his arm. The whole neighborhood comes to see what the ruckus was about, and he's running about, screaming flood. I have to run out of there in nothing but my braies. My braies. And with those burns, I can't even sit for a week. True story," said Nikola. Although the boy did not see what was so funny about this story, Nikola was laughing so hard tears were coming down his cheeks. "This'll be our campsite, then," he said.

Up ahead, two of the men were already starting to tie up the mules. The rest of the men unloaded all the strongboxes and stacked them up, all except for Nikola's. Nikola took his strongbox to the middle of camp and kept it by him while he watched the cook build a fire and prepare the rabbit stew. When it was done, the cook ladled out a bowlful for each man.

The men were not shy about eating, but they did stop to talk to each other or take swigs from their wineskins. Spurred by his hunger, the boy bolted the stew down. "That was good. Thank you, sir," he said to the cook.

The cook merely grunted in response.

"Go on and give him another bowl," said Nikola, looking up from his own.

"Just be wasting it," said the cook.

Nikola stared at the cook. "Give him another bowl," he said. The cook shrugged and ladled up another bowl of stew. The boy wolfed this one down as well. "Another bowl," said Nikola.

The cook said, "Sir—"

"Again," said Nikola. The cook ladled up a third bowl. "Eat up, son," said Nikola. "A little meat on those bones would profit us all." So the boy ate.

After dinner, Nikola told more of his stories, and the men joined in with some of their own. The boy lay back on a spare blanket and felt the shape of his stomach. His belly was so full of food that it was tender and swollen.

When the men began to bunk down for the night, the boy said, "I don't want to be just a burden. I'd like to help with the caravan."

"You'll be help enough when we get to the mine," said Nikola, lying back on his own blanket.

"I could keep one of the watches," said the boy, though as soon as he said it, he realized that no watch had been posted.

Nikola chuckled. "Lad, you don't have to guard the caravan on the way *to* the silver mine," he said. Then he rolled over and went to sleep.

♠

The dragon sat up on his hind legs like a dog. He loomed in close enough for Plain Alice to smell his sulfurous breath. "I hope I did not injure you," he said. The dragon spoke with a clipped, educated accent that did not match his immense, scaly bulk.

"What do you care if I am hurt, you monster?" said Plain Alice, still trying to get over the discovery that he could speak at all.

The dragon sniffed a little at that. "You humans slaughter each other with glee, but we dragons are the monsters? Dragons or men, who do you suppose has more blood on their claws, Alice?"

"That's not fair," said Plain Alice. "And since you know my name, you should at least tell me yours."

"My name is Ludwig," said the dragon. "And do forgive me. I did not realize you were blind."

That confused Plain Alice. "I'm not blind," she said. "I can see just fine."

That confused Ludwig back. "But you cannot see my name?" he asked.

"Of course not," said Plain Alice. "Wait, do you actually see people's names?"

"Yes," said Ludwig. "People, animals, objects, everything. How else would I avoid crashing into things?"

"What's the name of this rock?" asked Plain Alice, pointing at the basalt column.

Ludwig said, "It is called—" Then he emitted a kind of rumbly noise, so low that Plain Alice almost couldn't hear it. "It doesn't really translate."

"And the ground?" said Plain Alice.

"The patch of ground the rock sits on is—" He made a slightly different low, rumbly noise. "And far beneath it is a lava flow called—" This time, he put a little gurgling sound into the low rumble.

Plain Alice said, "What about—"

Ludwig cut her off with a wave of his claw. "What is it that *you* see?"

"I see, um . . . what things look like," said Plain Alice. Even as she spoke, she knew what she said was of no use to Ludwig. Words always went back to something that had been experienced before. She could describe what a particular thing looked like, but not what it was to see things. “When I look at something, I see, you know, its shape and color,” she said.

Only Ludwig did not know. “Does everything have these shapes and colors?” he asked.

“Yes,” said Plain Alice. Then, “No. Some things don’t, like air, but you can’t see them.” Then she thought about how in the summer, waves of heat coming from the ground could make things in the distance waver. “Well, sometimes you sort of can because they make other things change their shape.” And different kinds of light could change something’s color, too. “Or color.”

“Wait, if a thing changes shape and color, how can you ever know if you have seen it before?” asked Ludwig.

“Well, they don’t change shape and color that much, and it’s almost always when they’re far away,” said Plain Alice. Then she remembered about mirages. “Only sometimes, you see things that aren’t there at all.”

“That all sounds very confusing,” said Ludwig.

She would never be able to explain what she saw to Ludwig, and he would never be able to explain what he saw to her. Even though Ludwig saw things as words, he could not use words to tell her what it was like to see them. Ludwig would need a way to communicate that went beyond words, the ability to put the experience directly in her head. Much as she wanted to understand what Ludwig saw, she would never be able to. What they could not talk about, they would have to remain silent about.

"We dragons see everything that is, we know what it is and we see nothing that is not. Clearly, our way of seeing is better," said Ludwig. "Now, I should be able to let you go soon, but in the meantime, do humans eat mutton?"

"You're going to let me go?" said Plain Alice. "I was worried you might want to, well, devour me or something."

Ludwig made a face and gagged a little at the thought. "No, no, nothing like that. I have been summoned by a sorcerer and am subject to his will," said Ludwig.

"How did he get this power over you?" said Plain Alice.

"There is a ceremony, a secret rite. At the end of it, he burned my mark into his flesh. Until it fades, no one can free me from his command," said Ludwig.

"And he ordered you to kidnap me?" said Plain Alice. "What would some sorcerer want with me?"

"I am afraid I cannot say. All very hush-hush. Always is when it comes to power politics," said Ludwig.

"I'm not sure I believe that," said Plain Alice.

"You can believe what you like about the sun, but it will still rise tomorrow," said Ludwig.

"That's not really true," said Plain Alice. "The sun doesn't rise. The world turns to reveal the sun. It only looks like it's rising because of where we're standing." Plain Alice had been studying with her father to prepare for the next agon. She had just completed astronomy.

Ludwig wrinkled his brow and studied her a little more closely. "You're an educated girl, then?" he said.

"I study a bit," said Plain Alice.

"I, myself, am a student," said Ludwig. "I am a doctoral candidate in draconic sciences. I was about to present my dissertation when I was dragged off here to be the errand boy of some politically ambitious thug."

Plain Alice couldn't imagine who would go to the trouble of kidnapping her. Ludwig's little hints about politics were not helping, either. "What's your dissertation about?" she asked. She wanted to get on Ludwig's good side, and experience had taught her that the easiest way to get on a scholar's good side was to ask about his research.

"Well, it is a bit complicated. It is primarily about how to get around the cube-square law, but there is also some material about defying the laws of aerodynamics," said Ludwig. He looked at her hopefully.

Plain Alice did not know what any of that meant. "Bit over my head," she said.

"Yes, well, it is an advanced course of study," said Ludwig. "What about you? What do you study?"

"I'm apprenticed as a sage to my father," said Plain Alice. "Or, well, I'm going to be. I hope."

"What is the problem?" said Ludwig. "Is your father reluctant to take you on?"

"Oh, it's not him," said Plain Alice. "It's the Council of Sages. In order to be apprenticed as a sage, you have to win an ordinary. It's like a prize or an award; they give it to you for doing well at an agon. That's a kind of contest where there's a series of tricks and logic puzzles to solve. Winning an ordinary is supposed to show that you're clever enough to be a sage."

"And you have not won an ordinary yet?" asked the dragon.

"No, the Council won't invite me to compete," said Plain Alice. "Although I suppose, technically, that does mean: yes, I haven't won one yet."

"And there is no other way to become a sage?" said Ludwig.

"No," said Plain Alice. "Well, if you solve a big enough problem or mystery outside of an agon, you can ask the Council to approve that instead. That's called an extraordinary, but no one's won one of those in years and years."

"The answer seems obvious enough," said Ludwig. "If your problem is how to become an apprentice sage, and you can do that by winning an extraordinary, then all you have to do is point out to the Council that winning an extraordinary is the solution to the problem. Then they give you an extraordinary for solving the problem."

"And you think you're the first one to come up with that, do you?" said Plain Alice.

"Not when you ask the question like that, no," said Ludwig.

"It has to be an original solution," explained Plain

Alice, "which basically means it has to be a new problem."

"My dissertation committee is very picky, too," said Ludwig. "I have managed them, so I can probably manage your Council. With some thought, I should be able to think of a good problem for you to solve when you go home." He nodded. "In the meantime, if you will excuse me, I have some villagers to terrorize." So saying, Ludwig leapt back into the sky. The draft from his wings blasted her with sand and grit.

As soon as he had gone, she started to think of how to get down and, once she got down, how to find fresh water. Of course, she would also have to find her way back to civilization. It would be dangerous, but she had little choice. Ludwig might intend to let her go, but Plain Alice had less faith in the goodwill of evil sorcerers.

"Boy." The voice came in the middle of the night. "Boy."

"Master?" said the boy, snapping awake. He jumped to his feet and glanced around wildly. The silvery light of the near-full moon lit the camp. Nothing moved. No one was there. Casimir had not come to burn him. His heart slowed its thudding. "Who is it?" said the boy, wondering if he had simply dreamed the voice.

"Over here, in the box," said the voice.

The boy crept over to Nikola's strongbox. "That can't

be. It's too small," said the boy. The box was barely big enough to hold a small child, but the voice that came from it was a grown man's.

"Open it and take a look," said the voice.

The strongbox and its secret belonged to Nikola, and Nikola had taken the boy in and fed him. Respecting Nikola's secrets was a good way to repay his food and his company. So he would only take a quick peek. The boy lifted the strongbox's lid and peered inside. Two glowing yellow eyes stared out at him. The boy jumped back, dropping the lid and very nearly screaming.

"I said to take a look, not a glimpse," said the voice. A note of irritation crept into it.

The boy started to reach for the lid again but stopped himself. Whatever was in the box might be dangerous. He knew the wiser course was to leave well enough alone, but he was curious. Besides, he told himself, how much trouble could something so small cause? He threw the lid wide open.

The creature was fearfully strange-looking and dressed all in rags. His body was tiny and spindly, no bigger than a toddler's, and his skin was green, a green so dark it looked near purple in the moonlight. He had an elongated triangular head with two enormous oblong yellow eyes, slit down the middle like a cat's. His long, pointy ears stuck up above the crown of his head, and his wide mouth was filled with hundreds of needle-sharp teeth.

"Good evening, kind sir," said the creature. He spoke in a whisper. "As you are obviously a refined gentleman of noble character, I do hope you might forgive me for the imposition of introducing myself without a proper letter of reference. Please feel free to call me Mennofar."

The boy stared at Mennofar.

"I see that look in your eye, and you are quite right, clever lad that you are. That would be quite a short name for a goblin. Mennofar, you see, is only a nickname," said Mennofar. "But as my full name is over forty-seven thousand syllables long and takes a full four hours to recite, I am willing to allow certain liberties, such as the use of my nickname. Especially as we are in a bit of a hurry."

The boy continued to stare.

"To escape, lad," said Mennofar. "We are in a hurry to effect my escape."

"You're a goblin," said the boy.

"The keenness of your mind is a wonderment," said Mennofar.

But the boy was not being stupid. He was racking his brain to remember everything he could about goblins from The Tales. Goblins were magical creatures with all manner of powers. They knew all things, past and future. And he was pretty sure they granted wishes, though that might have been genies or magic rings or talking fish or something. It seemed like there might have been something about buried treasure, too. But goblins were troublesome creatures. On this, The Tales were quite clear. They loved to tell lies and trick people. And though goblins never, ever broke a promise, they made all kinds of trouble by scrupulously enforcing their word to the letter.

No matter how hard the boy thought, he could remember nothing from The Tales about goblins in strongboxes. Finally, he said, "What're you doing in there?"

"Relatively little, as I am being held prisoner by our mutual acquaintance," said Mennofar, nodding his head toward Nikola. "Hence the need to escape."

The boy said, "But why—"

"It is a long story," said Mennofar. "One that I would be happy to relate with great animation and marginal accuracy at some later date. But for now, I would very much appreciate it if you would see about freeing me." Then, before the boy could stare at him some more, he added, "The key lies on a chain around Nikola's neck."

The boy peered down into the strongbox. Mennofar's ankles and wrists were bound in iron shackles that kept him from moving. And around Nikola's neck was a key on a chain. The key rested on Nikola's chest. It rose and fell with his breathing. "Only how do I know Nikola doesn't have a good reason for keeping you locked up?" said the boy. "You might be evil."

"A sage inquiry. Nikola has imprisoned me in the hopes that I will grant him three wishes," said Mennofar, "which is once stupid because goblins do not grant wishes, we make vows, and twice stupid because a goblin's honor permits him to make these vows only to his rescuer, never to his captor." Mennofar gritted his teeth. "As I have explained to him many, many times."

"If he thinks you'll give him wishes, why doesn't he have you under guard?" said the boy.

"As long as I am locked in this thing"—he jostled the chains a little—"I cannot escape," said Mennofar. "Besides, he has had me in his power long enough to grow careless."

The shackles were brown with rust, and far too small to have been made for anyone but Mennofar. "How long have you been locked up?" said the boy.

"Nine years," said Mennofar. "We goblins are patient, and we live a long time."

"And you can't magic your way out or something?" said the boy. As soon as he said it, he knew the question was stupid. Plainly, he would have if he could have.

"No, iron is the bane of goblins," said Mennofar. "We have no power over it. Just its touch burns like hot coals."

The boy shuddered a little at the word "burn." He leaned forward and examined Mennofar's ankles and wrists. Wherever the iron touched, there were terrible burns and scars. It was a fearsome sight, and it made the guilt well up in the boy's chest again. He had defied the gods rather than burn for just a few minutes, but Mennofar had burned for nine years without giving in.

Rather than risk waking Nikola by trying to take the

key from around his neck, the boy lifted Mennofar out of the strongbox and carried him, chains and all, to the key.

With one arm, he held Mennofar over Nikola so that the padlock hung down only a few inches above the key. Mennofar was not heavy, even with the shackles, but holding him over Nikola's chest was awkward. The boy's arm began to tremble from the effort.

Concentrating on the rising and falling of Nikola's chest, the boy timed his moment. When Nikola's chest was at the top of one of its rises, the boy delicately closed his thumb and finger on the key. Nikola's chest sank back again, leaving the key in the boy's grasp. For one awful moment, Nikola began to stir. The boy froze. When Nikola did not wake, the boy lifted the key the few inches to the padlock and slid it in.

The lock turned easily and popped open. When the lock opened, its weight shifted, and it began to slide off the ring that secured it to the shackles. Mennofar winced, but the boy caught it just before it dropped onto Nikola's chest. Still trembling, the boy set Mennofar on the ground. He slid the key from the lock. Gently, he set the key back on Nikola's chest.

The boy carried Mennofar to the edge of the camp, where he undid the shackles. Mennofar and the boy just stared at each other for a moment. "Go on, then," said the boy. "Run."

Mennofar tried to raise his arm a little. It shook

violently from the effort. "My imprisonment has left me too weak to travel under my own power," he said. "Do not worry, though. I am very light. Even carrying me, a strapping physical specimen such as you should have no trouble escaping Nikola."

"Why do I want to escape from Nikola?" said the boy. "He took me in and fed me. He's a friend."

"Because your friend Nikola is going to sell you to the silver mines," said Mennofar.

"You're a liar," said the boy. He spoke as forcefully as he could to cover his own uncertainty. "Goblins are great ones for lying."

"Indeed, we take pride in it," said Mennofar. "But ask yourself, why would he take you in if not to sell you? Why would he feed you so well if not to get more coin for you?"

"Kindness?" said the boy.

"Though it pains me to taint the purity of such innocence, I feel obliged to point out that in this world, kindness, like the unicorn, is chiefly found in stories told to princesses," said Mennofar. "Ordinary folk look to how the coin falls."

The boy looked over at Nikola's face. Even asleep, the hard lines were there, lines that some might go so far as to call cruel. The boy wanted Nikola to be a friend, but friendly or not, he knew Nikola would never pass on silver.

He rubbed his father's ring between his fingers. Of

course, mine slavery just might be the answer to all his woes. Fate was a slippery thing. His fate was to be a slave, but maybe not Casimir's slave particularly. Perhaps he could let himself be sold to the mines, submit to the will of the gods and save himself from burning for his crimes. It was a hard solution, but one worth thinking over.

"What are you waiting for?" said Mennofar. "Do you want to be a slave?"

The boy scooped Mennofar up in his arms and ran.

4

Each morning, Ludwig brought Plain Alice a fresh bucket of water before flying off and leaving her atop the pillar all day. Plain Alice would eat the leftovers from the night before for breakfast and lunch. At dusk, Ludwig would return with a sheep for their dinner and cook it with his fiery breath. Though dinner was often half burnt and half raw, Plain Alice was always hungry enough to get it down. Her real enemies were boredom and worry. There was nothing to do but fret about her poor father. She knew he would be in a state.

On the fourth evening, Ludwig returned in a glum mood. As Plain Alice forced herself to eat another meal of charred mutton, he said, "I have been showing myself all across the country. Why haven't any knights or lords come to rescue you?"

"Why would they?" she asked.

"Whyever not?" asked Ludwig. "I have not taken the Introduction to Mankind class yet, but I'm pretty sure rescuing princesses is how knights and lords make their reputations."

In spite of her situation, Plain Alice burst out laughing. "You wanted *Princess* Alice?" she said. "Then you've kidnapped the wrong girl."

"But you are Alice," insisted Ludwig.

"The Princess and I are both named Alice," said Plain Alice.

Ludwig was shocked. "There are two people named Alice?" he said.

"A lot more than two. There are probably hundreds when you take in all of the Kingdoms. It's a fairly common name," said Plain Alice.

Ludwig's face sank. "Oh, but . . . but this is terrible," he said. "I have kidnapped the wrong girl."

"Think how I feel about it," said Plain Alice.

Ludwig cocked his head. "I suppose that is a fair point," he said. "Er, sorry."

Plain Alice should have been very angry, but Ludwig

said it with such innocence that she almost laughed. "It was an honest mistake," she said. "Just take me home, and I'll forgive you."

Ludwig looked down at his foreclaws. "Yes, about that . . ."

"What?" said Plain Alice.

"Only . . . you know how villains tend to feel about witnesses," he said. "I am not sure what I am supposed to do."

Until that moment, Ludwig had been quite kind to Plain Alice, but she didn't like where this conversation was going. "You could ask," she suggested. "Go and see him. I really don't know anything, so maybe he'll say you can let me go."

Ludwig lit up. "Yes, I am *sure* he will understand. I will go to him at once." He spread his great bat wings and launched himself into the air.

Plain Alice harbored none of Ludwig's illusions. She was sure the evil sorcerer, whoever he was, would say something like *Only the dead keep secrets.* That was the sort of thing evil sorcerers liked to say. She'd suggested Ludwig speak to his master only to give herself a chance to escape.

The nearest stone column was fifteen feet away, and it was also eight or nine feet down. With a running start, she might be able to make it that far. Or she might not. There was a reason she had not tried already. Still, the moment had come. Biting down hard on her fears, she ran and leapt into the open air. For a moment, she thought she was going to make it.

But only for a moment. As the column rose toward her, her stomach fell away. Her legs kicked uselessly at the open air. She struck the side of the column. The force knocked the wind from her, but she managed to get the tips of her fingers over the edge of the column.

She clung there, gasping, until she regained her breath. Then she slowly began to drag herself up over the lip. Her arms ached and shook with the effort of pulling herself up, but she finally got high enough that she could swing one leg, then the other, over the top. She flopped up onto the top of the column and lay there, wheezing. Her heart thudded in her chest. The sweat poured off her, chilling her.

The worst part was that she had to do it again. There was another column with another drop. This time, it was not quite so far away. She made the top of the column and even rolled out of the landing, although she nearly tumbled off the far side.

The third column was short enough to try for the ground. She lowered herself over the side and hung from the edge of the column. She took a moment to fill her heart with iron. Then she dropped. She landed hard enough to wind up flat on the ground, but she was unhurt. Standing and dusting herself off, she smiled. She was the daughter of a scholar and not an especially athletic girl, but she had gotten herself down unharmed.

She looked around. The Stanhope Road lay to the south. It was also the first direction Ludwig would look, but there was nothing for it. She was surrounded by wilderness. East lay the Mountains of Fire, the Spine was far to the north, and the Little Dismal swallowed the west. Knowing little of these places beyond their names, she would be lost in broken terrain almost at once. She headed south.

♠

Had Oswald lived a century ago, he would have gone east to Uskborough to present a petition to the royal court. Long before he was born, however, Queen Claudia, the wife of King Andreas VI of Stanhope, gave birth to twin boys. Even in those days, everyone knew twins were a bad omen, bringing nothing but misfortune and ill luck. Every sage and astrologer in the land advised the king to drown them both in a well, as tradition required. It really was the only civilized thing to do. But old King Andreas did not have the heart—or rather the lack of heart—to do it. He split Stanhope in two and left half to each of his sons instead. Ever since, West Stanhopers who wanted to petition the royal court had gone west to Farnham.

When Oswald left Middlebury, he took with him a letter of introduction from the Earl. To make sure the petition was taken seriously, the Earl also lent him his personal shield, Magan. Magan was painted with a blue griffin on a yellow field, the Earl's personal emblem. No one would dare carry her without the Earl's permission. The Earl also offered him a horse, but Oswald did not know how to ride. So he went on foot, carrying Magan across his back. She was one of those old-fashioned tower shields and weighed heavily on Oswald. By the end of the first morning, his shoulders were sore and raw from the rubbing of her traveling straps. When the pain grew great, he thought of Plain Alice and marched on.

The country between Middlebury and Farnham was full of farms and villages, and Oswald was able to spend the first two nights sleeping on benches in inns. The third night he spent on the ground by the side of the road. This made his hip hurt, but again, he marched through the pain.

Late on the fourth day, Oswald crested the final hill and saw Farnham for the first time in over a decade. Sitting on the edge of the plain that gently sloped down to the Western Ocean, it was a trim little city made up mostly of half-timbered buildings, some soaring as high as three stories. The upper floors jutted out over the narrow city streets below, sometimes almost meeting their neighbors across the way. The only substantial stone structures were the city walls and the royal palace, which sat on a rise in the middle of town. As capitals went, Farnham was more quaint and sleepy than fearsome and mighty. Of course, it had simply been the largest port town in the west of Stanhope until the role of capital was suddenly, some might even say rudely, thrust upon it. It had yet to grow into its new role.

Oswald arrived just as the watch was closing the city gates. Once they were closed, no one was allowed in or out until the next morning. Oswald used Magan to jam the gate open just long enough to make it through. The watchmen were unhappy, but the Earl's shield kept them from arresting Oswald. Magan herself suffered two crunch marks to her rim. Oswald had no time to worry about the damage and hustled off to the royal palace instead.

When Stanhope was first divided in half, a new royal palace was needed in a hurry, so the old customs house had been renovated and expanded in a rush. Every expense had been spared, and the result was a curiously ugly mix of warehouse and semi-fortified manor home that was neither pleasant to live in nor particularly siege-proof.

Not satisfied with being an uncomfortable and insecure eyesore, the palace eventually began to actively threaten the lives of its occupants. It developed the alarming habit of shedding heavy stone gargoyles at awkward moments. Nearly thirty-five years before, on the eve of his wedding, just such a gargoyle landed on the head of Crown Prince Baldwin, which is how his younger brother, Julian II, wound up being king instead of Baldwin.

The decades since had seen no improvements in upkeep, so when Oswald laid eyes on it, it looked as tatty and run-down as ever. It also looked like it was shut up for the night. Oswald pounded on the doors of the main entrance. "Open up. Open up," he cried. "I must see the King." He sounded unhinged, but he carried on pounding.

A tiny slot in the door slid open. It was just large enough for two eyes to glare out at him. "Go away," said the eyes.

"I bear an urgent message from the Earl of Middlebury," said Oswald.

"Then bear it another time," said the eyes. "Come back in the morning." The slot slammed shut again.

"Please, please open up," cried Oswald. "My daughter has been stolen by a dragon." The sound of boots clomping off told him there was no point in pleading further. For several long minutes, Oswald simply stood there. He might not be able to go on, but he would not go back. If he had to, he would spend the night at the palace gates. No sooner had he begun to look for a soft spot to lie down than the slot opened up again. "From the Earl of Middlebury, you said?" said the eyes.

Oswald said, "Yes, and—"

"Wait there." The slot closed. The boots thumped away again. It was several minutes before the click-clack of shoes arrived. The palace doors flew open. On the other side was a pinch-faced man in a powdered wig, striped trousers and a frock coat that had gotten a little shiny at the elbows. His shoulders were covered in the cheaper kind of wig powder, the stuff that never adhered properly, and he wore the type of shiny black patent leather shoes with silver buckles that always pinch the wearer's feet terribly. "I am the Bailiff to His Majesty Julian the Second, Monarch of West Stanhope and Lord of All Its Assorted Dependencies," he said. "All royal business must be transacted through me. Now, what message from the Right Honorable the Earl of Middlebury do you bear for His Majesty?"

Oswald studied the Bailiff. He was plainly the sort of fellow who felt his duty was to keep everyone away from the King. If Oswald told him anything, he would shunt Oswald off to a room somewhere and make him wait, possibly forever. "I am Oswald the Sage. Lord Middlebury commanded me to deliver the letter to His Majesty personally," said Oswald, which was a bit of an exaggeration. "Then I am to give him a message too sensitive to be written down," he added, an outright lie.

The Bailiff pursed his lips. "Well, I am sure Lord Middlebury merely meant that it should not go to anyone short of the royal cabinet, of which I am the relevant and appropriate officer. So—"

"To His Majesty *personally.* On that point his Lordship was quite clear," said Oswald. "He did allow me to say that it concerns the security of the realm."

At that, the Bailiff pursed his lips still tighter. He took a long moment to look Oswald over from head to toe.

In response, Oswald unslung the shield and showed it to him. "Yes, yes," said the Bailiff. "Come with me."

Oswald followed the Bailiff into the courtyard. Halfway across, the Bailiff stopped and studied the roofline of the main hall. Then he dashed the rest of the way across the courtyard to the entrance of the hall. When he saw that Oswald had stopped to stare, the Bailiff impatiently waved at him to follow. Not quite sure why, Oswald dashed across the courtyard, too. When he got to the entrance, the Bailiff said, "Better safe than sorry."

♠

The boy ran deep into the foothills. He ran away from Nikola and the road, away from Tibor and Rodrigo, away from Casimir and the whole of the world he had known. With his way lit by the near-full moon, he ran for what seemed like hours. All the while, he carried Mennofar draped around his neck like a shepherd carrying a lamb. When he had run as long and hard as he could, he flopped down on the ground, panting.

Mennofar dragged himself over to a rock and propped himself up against it. Closing his eyes tightly, he leaned his head forward.

"I do all the work, and you take a nap," said the boy.

"A little silence, please," said Mennofar. "I need to concentrate." He sat in silence for a moment more. Then he opened his eyes. "At this distance, we should be safe enough. They will pursue us, but they will give up long before coming this far. Deep down, Nikola knows I will never give in to his demands, and he will not risk his schedule for the few florins you might bring him."

"That's certain?" said the boy.

"Certain as the future can ever be," said Mennofar.

"So it's true what they say about goblins?" said the boy. "You do know all things, past and future?"

"It is true after a fashion, but I do not know all things the way you know something you are taught or something you remember. I have to look for them with my third eye," said Mennofar, tapping the middle of his forehead. "It is like being in a room with a window. You can look out the window whenever you want, but until you do, you do not know what is there. If I want to see something with my third eye, I must search it out."

"And you can see past, present and future, all the same?" said the boy.

"Not all the same," said Mennofar. "The past is written in stone, but the future is written in water. Each choice makes a new future, though some choices make more difference than others. I can see all of these futures come and go. By watching how the futures fold back into one another, I gain a sense of how likely each one is."

"Forever?" asked the boy.

"As I look further into the future, the number of possibilities multiplies, and the chance of each one coming to pass declines," said Mennofar. "Eventually, there are too many possibilities to make sense of. It is like trying to pick out a single leaf in a tree. If you are close, it is easy. The farther away you get, the harder it is. Far enough, and the tree is just a mass of green, no matter how hard you look at it."

"And does your third eye say where we can get food?" said the boy. In his rush to get away, he had not thought to bring any supplies.

"I do not need a third eye to answer that. You tear a sleeve off your tunic and make a slingshot of it. Use it to hunt," said Mennofar.

The boy looked at the scrubby and desolate hills around them. "For what?" he said.

"Bats," said Mennofar. He smiled, exposing his many sharp little teeth. "Wherever there are mountains, there are bats. You will go bat hunting." The boy made a face. "No need to be like that. Bats are really quite tasty."

That seemed unlikely, but the boy did not argue. He was going to eat those bats whether they were tasty or no. That was life, eating what was to be had.

5

Ludwig was only a small gray spot in the sky when Plain Alice spotted him. She stopped and watched. At first, he was headed toward her, but then he turned and flew a ways across her trail. Then he turned and disappeared in the opposite direction.

She stood at the foot of the mountains and watched for a few more minutes. It did not seem possible. He could not be giving up that easily. She was about to turn to go when she saw him again. He was coming toward her once more. He came closer this time, but then he turned again.

That was when she knew: he was hunting for her by flying in ever-broader circles. Fast. She ran toward the swamp. She told herself that if she could just get under cover, she would be safe. But the nearest tree was still half a mile away. She ran and ran and ran, only to have the ground fall away sickeningly when Ludwig snatched her up once again.

"I told him what happened, and he laughed," said Ludwig. "He thought it was very funny."

"Nasty man," said Plain Alice. "What did he tell you to do with me?"

"You'll know soon enough," said Ludwig.

He might have been trying to protect her from the truth, but his silence only made things worse. Being set adrift, far out to sea, or dashed onto rocks or dropped into a volcano—all manner of terrible fates sprang to mind. None of them included being set down in a clearing in the middle of the Little Dismal.

"I'm very sorry," said Ludwig. A great tear began to pool in the corner of his eye.

He looked so miserable that Plain Alice reached out and patted him on his snout. "It's all right," she said. "Whatever this is, I will survive it."

"I hope so," said Ludwig, "but I fear not." Then he was in the sky once more. As she watched him leave, she marveled that such a huge creature could fly so beautifully and naturally.

Then she turned to her own situation. The only

thing in the clearing was a tiny windowless wooden hut, built entirely of raw logs. It was too small for a home, but she could not think what other purpose it might have.

Things did not seem so terrible. They had not flown over the Stanhope Road, which meant it was south of her. She could use the sun to keep a generally southern path until she found the road. She should be able to make her way home.

Before she could get her bearings, a huge brutish creature nearly ten feet tall broke out of the tree line. He looked something like a man, but lumpy and misshapen, as if a child had made him out of clay. His skin was an unpleasant shade of pale gray. His small, dim eyes were sunk deep in their sockets. His mouth had a collection of teeth that looked as if they had been casually tossed in there. His head was completely bald, but there were odd patches of wiry black hair in random spots on his body. The ogre, for that was what he was, wore the skins of animals, but not sewn into clothing. Instead, the hides were simply tied to his body haphazardly.

Something so large should not have been able to move so quickly, but he did. No sooner was he out of the trees than he had Plain Alice in his meaty grip. "Dragon leave me present?" he asked.

"Yes, he thought we could be friends," she said. It was a long shot, but ogres were notoriously stupid creatures.

The ogre leaned in close, putting his nose almost directly into her hair. He sniffed deeply. "Mmm, girl," he said. "Like girls."

"And I like ogres, though I never met one before," said Plain Alice.

"Girls yummiest of all," said the ogre. Then he popped her into the hut and bolted the door behind her. Inside, the bones revealed the hut's purpose: it was a larder.

♠

Oswald followed the Bailiff down a long passage to a large set of double doors that opened onto the royal library. There, King Julian was meeting with all the members of the cabinet except the Royal Astrologer. Falling statuary had created an unexpected job opening. The surviving members of the cabinet were resplendent in velvet waistcoats, silk cravats, jeweled stickpins and powdered wigs. These wigs increased in size and complexity with the rank of the officers wearing them. The King's own wig was so large that he could not actually wear it. It sat next to him, in its own chair.

"Your Majesty," intoned the Bailiff, "may I present Oswald the Sage, of Middlebury, emissary of Your Right Trusty and Well-Beloved Cousin, the Right Honorable the Earl of Middlebury, who bears a message for Your Royal Personage."

♠

King Julian looked up. Any interruption of this meeting was most welcome. The cabinet had come to the King because they felt it was time to find Princess Alice a husband, ideally one with a lot of money. King Julian loved his daughter, even if her giggling annoyed him. He did not want to make her marry someone for his money, but he had long since learned that being king mostly meant doing things you didn't want to do. And there was no getting around it: West Stanhope was broke. The royal budget was devoured by army pay, castle maintenance, the costs of the royal court, salaries for the civil servants and the endlessly rising price of wig powder. On top of that, there was the cost of applying to the High King for permission to change the law and make the Princess heir to the throne.

From his court in the Imperial City, the High King ruled nearly the whole of the world, which included dozens of kingdoms, principalities, grand duchies, sovereign margraviates, autonomous city-states, overseas exarchates and so on and so on. Obviously, it could prove challenging for any one monarch to get his attention. Still, every year King Julian sent a raft of functionaries and sages and astrologers and lawyers to attend the court of the High King. And every year, they petitioned and attested and forecasted and pettifogged (and bribed) the officers of the High King's court in an effort to get permission to change the law. But Duke Geoffrey had functionaries and sages and astrologers and lawyers to petition and attest and forecast and pettifog (and bribe), too. So every year, there was some new reason why the matter would have to be put off another year. Slow as this was, King Julian would never give up. It was his sworn duty to protect the people, and that included protecting them from the likes of Duke Geoffrey.

In the meantime, West Stanhope sank deeper and deeper in debt.

Had Duke Geoffrey been king, he would have solved the problem by taxing the people ruthlessly, but then Duke Geoffrey would have been an oppressive tyrant. That was the reason King Julian was trying so hard to keep him off the throne in the first place. It was also the reason King Julian could not pursue a policy of ruthless taxation. There was no point in saving the people from an oppressive tyrant if he had to tyrannize them oppressively to do it. The cabinet's answer was for Princess Alice to marry a wealthy prince. Much as King Julian hated it, he had yet to think of a better solution.

"Gentlemen," said King Julian. "It looks like we will have to set aside this discussion for now."

The Minister of the Treasury said, "But, Your Majesty, the kingdom is running out of money."

"Then we can defer the maintenance work on the palace until next year," said King Julian. "That should loosen up a few coins."

The members of the cabinet turned pale: they all

worked in the palace. "There are safety concerns," said the Chamberlain. He looked over at the Royal Astrologer's empty chair.

"We just have to muddle through somehow," said King Julian. "Isn't that our motto?" (Technically, West Stanhope's motto was *"Permuddlare necesse est,"* these things sounding better in Latin.)

The members of the cabinet all nodded gravely.

"There you go," said King Julian. He looked to Oswald and then to Magan's familiar griffin. "Now, Oswald, Sage of Middlebury, what has Godric to say?"

Oswald bowed a little. No sooner did he take a step forward to deliver the message than the letter was snatched by the Bailiff, who handed it to the Tipstaff, who carried it to the Steward. The Steward checked that it was properly addressed and gave it to the Seneschal, who inspected the seal. The Seneschal carried it past the Minister of the Treasury, who scowled—unhappy that he did not have an excuse to inspect the letter—and gave it to the Captain of the Guard, who shook it a few times to confirm that it did not pose a threat and then handed it to the Chamberlain, who broke the seal, opened it and offered it to King Julian.

"You must forgive us for some of our more burdensome procedures," said King Julian. He put on his reading glasses and looked at the letter. "Godric attests to your good character and says that you have a tale for me."

"Your Majesty, I have come to plead with you to dispatch knights and men-at-arms to rescue my daughter," said Oswald. "She was carried away by a dragon." While he spoke, the Minister of the Treasury looked off into the distance, and the Captain of the Guard rolled his eyes.

"I see," said King Julian. This was trouble. A marauding beast meant he would have to offer a reward, and if the beast was a dragon, the reward would have to be substantial.

The Chamberlain shifted in his chair. "Your Majesty is not, I hope, taking this seriously?" he asked.

"Shouldn't I?" said King Julian.

"Your Majesty, this report might sound compelling, but it is important to know how reliable the source is," said the Bailiff.

"The source?" said King Julian. "This man is the source, and he says he saw a dragon."

"Unreliable hearsay, Your Majesty," spluttered the Tipstaff. "The suggestion should be dismissed out of hand."

"And what of the security risk?" said the Captain of the Guard. "If we send all of our men off to chase some delusion, we will have nothing to defend the kingdom from her enemies"—here he paused and glanced about meaningfully—"both external and *internal.*" The Captain of the Guard was big on questions of internal security.

Oswald said, "It is not a delusion. I saw—"

"Your Majesty," said the Seneschal. "What if the army has to leave West Stanhope to catch the dragon? We will need to consult with the court of the High King in the Imperial City." Whatever it was, the Seneschal always said they would need to consult with the High King. It was the perfect objection. It took months, and there was never a definite answer.

"And think of the expense, Your Majesty," said the Minister of the Treasury. "It will cost a fortune." As Minister of the Treasury, he had a good objection to anything. Whatever it was, West Stanhope could not afford it.

Not wanting to be left out, the Steward shot out of his chair. "Your Majesty should also be concerned about, um . . . um . . ." Unable to think of an objection of his own, he stammered along until he realized that the Chamberlain was glaring at him. Turning beet red, he quickly finished up with, "Um . . . other problems that might come up." He shrank back into his chair.

The Chamberlain slowly rose to his feet. "I think Your Majesty can see that hasty action, particularly action based on reports of questionable reliability"—he eyed Oswald doubtfully—"may be problematic. Perhaps Your Highness might appoint a panel of experts to study all the possible courses of action, including the potential need to consult the court of the High King." He let a favorable eye fall on the Seneschal, while the Steward turned even redder.

"You want a panel?" said the King. "To study whether there are dragons?"

"To study whether there are dragons in West Stanhope, Your Majesty," said the Chamberlain.

"Go on," said the King.

"Once the panel makes its report," said the Chamberlain, "Your Majesty can be confident of making the best possible decision."

The King fixed the Chamberlain with a mighty stare. Then he turned to Oswald and said, "It's going to be a challenge, but if I fight with this lot all night, I may be able to get a rescue effort off by the morning." He waved to the Bailiff. "Find this man a room and a meal."

The door to the library banged open. Queen Ludmilla charged into the room. Behind her was a train of ladies-in-waiting, all wheezing and perspiring with unaccustomed effort. The members of the cabinet all jumped to their feet and bowed deeply. She ignored them all. "Oh, Julie, it's Alice!" she cried. Tears stained her cheeks. "She's been kidnapped!"

All of his old concerns—whom the Princess might marry, whether she would be serious enough to rule one day, what was behind all that giggling—every single one of these problems became nothing. "From inside the palace?" said the King. "By whom? How is it even possible?"

"She's been carried off by a dragon."

♠

The boy stopped to rest again at midday. When he put Mennofar down, he saw that Mennofar's skin had gone from an unpleasant inky-dark green to a healthier-looking forest green. Odder still, he was no longer dressed in rags. Instead, he wore a neatly tailored traveling suit.

"Where'd you get those clothes?" said the boy.

"It is a raiment," said Mennofar. Then, seeing that this did not help, he added, "Magical clothing. It fashions itself into whatever seems most appropriate under the circumstances."

"It's hardly fair, you knowing all," said the boy. "I have to ask you everything, and you don't have to ask me anything."

They both sat in silence for a moment.

"Why did you do it?" asked Mennofar. "Set me free like that?"

"I don't know," said the boy. And he truly did not. He did not know why he did most of the things he did. He tried to think things through carefully, but somehow he wound up doing the first thing that popped into his head. It was part of the reason he was such a bad slave. "Maybe I was just being friendly."

"It is hard for a goblin and a human to be friends," said Mennofar. "Goblin honor and human honor are so very different."

"Slaves have no honor," said the boy. Everyone knew that. "Anyway, those chains looked like they hurt."

"They did," said Mennofar.

"Well, that's why I freed you, then. I couldn't just let you burn like that," said the boy.

"But you did not try to get me to make any vows," said Mennofar. "I even gave you hints."

"That doesn't seem right, demanding vows when I was going to do it anyway. Wouldn't have been fair," said the boy, though that made it sound like he had thought things through.

"Not fair? Not fair?" said Mennofar. "Life is not fair. You are a slave. How is that fair?"

"It's my fate," said the boy.

"Yes, but how can having such a fate be fair?" said Mennofar, just as if he were making a good point.

"The Three Sisters draw all fates from the same bowl. My chances were the same as anyone else's," said the boy. "What could be more just?"

Mennofar shook his head, but he let the matter drop. "Would you count it fair to accept the vows now?" said Mennofar.

"Like a reward?" said the boy.

"Absolutely not," said Mennofar. "That would be an egregious violation of the goblin code of honor. I can grant vows only under duress. Even then, I must try to torment the person I make my vows to by giving those vows the strictest, most exacting interpretation possible. Anything less would be a permanent stain on my character, and I would be cast out of goblin society forever."

"It's dishonorable to reward someone who helps you?" asked the boy.

"Yes, it is," said Mennofar. He tapped his nose and dropped his voice. "I did warn you that a goblin's honor is very different from a human's. Now, do you want my vows or not?"

The boy studied Mennofar. It could be a trick. "How can you give me a vow now? I've already rescued you," he said.

"A fine point," said Mennofar. "But as I am still physically helpless and will need your help to survive until I heal, a case could be made that you have not actually finished rescuing me yet." He leaned in. "Just for purposes of reference, you should know that three is the customary number of vows for rescuing a goblin."

The offer was tempting but frightening. Goblins were notoriously tricksome. The Tales warned of men who came a cropper for dealing with them casually. Of course, such a vow would be valuable. Too valuable for a slave. "I am Casimir's slave," said the boy. "Any reward would rightly belong to him." He'd already cheated his master out of a slave. He didn't want to make his crimes any worse.

"You risked your life to save me," said Mennofar. "I wish to reward—er, show my recognition of that to you, not ratty old Casimir."

"The life I risked belongs to Casimir," said the boy.

"Ah, but the vows will make you a more valuable slave," said Mennofar. "Like putting fresh whitewash on a house."

Only a fool would fall for that one. "No, you must give those vows to Casimir," said the boy.

"Here is my final offer: I will give you two of the vows and save one for Casimir. If ever I happen upon the man, I will give him any vow you want."

The boy hesitated.

Mennofar smiled a little. His skin turned a lighter shade of green. "Casimir gets a vow, if you accept. If you refuse, he gets nothing. Now, would a good slaveboy cheat his master of something as valuable as a goblin's vow?" he said.

Goblins, it turned out, were just as clever and tricky as everyone said. "Two for Casimir and one for me," said the boy. Maybe if Casimir got more than the boy, he wouldn't be *too* angry.

"Believe me when I tell you that two may not be quite enough," said Mennofar. "So take your two vows. Otherwise, Casimir gets nothing."

"I accept," said the boy. He could always lie and say he'd gotten only one.

"Wonderful," said Mennofar. "Well?"

"Give me a minute. I have to think about what to ask for," said the boy.

"No, no, no, no," said Mennofar. "You must subject me to duress before extracting the vows from me."

"How do I do that?" asked the boy. This whole business was terribly complicated.

"A more creative lad would have no trouble devising

several possibilities, but threatening to leave me here to starve should suffice," said Mennofar.

"Fine," said the boy through gritted teeth. "Mennofar, give me the vows, or I'll leave you here."

"Weak," said Mennofar. "Not even remotely credible."

This was getting ridiculous. "That's it," said the boy. "If you don't knock this off right now, I will leave you here." He stood up. "And you can starve, for all I care."

"Oooh, that is much better," said Mennofar. Quite suddenly, he began to weep piteously. "No, you cannot," he cried out, "for I would die, and I will do anything to prevent that."

The boy glanced around to see if they were going through all of this for the benefit of someone else, but there was no one. "Will you give me three vows, two for me and one for my master, Casimir?"

"Yes, yes," said Mennofar. He stopped crying. "It took you a moment, but you were very good once you got going. I very nearly believed you would leave me."

"Did we really need to do all that?"

"Absolutely. Abandon all of life's little rituals, and you descend into barbarism," said Mennofar. "Now, what is your first vow?" He rubbed his hands together in excitement.

"I want you to vow to always help me in any way you can," said the boy.

"No," said Mennofar.

"No? You can say no?"

"If the vow is unduly onerous," said Mennofar. "Help you in any way I can? Such as washing all your clothes for you? Cutting up your meals? Cleaning your feet when they get dirty? It would very nearly turn *me* into a slave."

"I didn't mean it like that," said the boy. "I only wanted you to help with the big things in life."

"And how am I to judge when something is one of 'the big things in life'?" said Mennofar. "And while you are thinking about that, I will also need to know how much effort I should put into helping you. Or were you expecting me to work myself to death?"

When the boy said it, he'd known what he meant. He just wanted Mennofar to help him, though not in some tricksy way that made things worse. The trouble was that Mennofar was right. Just saying "the big things in life" was too vague.

"I want you to vow to help me prove my innocence to Casimir," said the boy. That way he could go home.

"An excellent choice," said Mennofar. "Boy who rescued me, I, Mennofar the Goblin, vow—"

"Wait. Stop," said the boy. "You're just going to do the tiniest little thing that helps in some way that barely matters, aren't you?"

"There is my honor to consider," said Mennofar.

"And if I ask you to vow to help a lot, you'll say that's too vague," said the boy.

"Yes," said Mennofar. "I mean, if you are willing to let me be the judge of what constitutes 'a lot,' then—"

"No," said the boy. What he needed was some way to make Mennofar useful without leaving him any wiggle room. "You know everything, right?" said the boy. "I want you to vow never to lie to me."

"Now, that *is* an excellent choice," said Mennofar. "Boy who rescued me, I, Mennofar the Goblin, vow that I shall never lie to you."

"Where can I find buried treasure?" asked the boy. If he brought home a big enough treasure, Casimir would forgive him for not helping Tibor and running away. Well, maybe. At the very least, Casimir would only have the boy's ears cut off. Either way, the boy could go back to being a slave without being burned alive.

Mennofar looked at the boy in perfect innocence. He said nothing.

"Answer the question," said the boy.

"No," said Mennofar.

"But you have to," said the boy. "You promised."

"I did no such thing," said Mennofar. "I promised only that I would not lie. When I choose to speak, the words I speak will be true."

It was another trick, but it was a good one. Mennofar's vow didn't compel him to say anything at all. There was a simple enough solution to that. "Then, for my second vow, I want you to answer every question I put to you," said the boy.

"No," said Mennofar. "That also goes too far. I would be willing to take a vow to answer a single yes-or-no question each day."

"That's it? One yes-or-no question a day?" said the boy.

Mennofar smiled. "Whose rules are these?" he asked. "Anyway, giving everything away all at once spoils the fun."

There had to be a trick to that, too. "How long do I get? The rest of my life?" he asked.

"Or until the third vow is made," said Mennofar.

It was the best he was going to do. "I'll take it," said the boy.

"Boy who rescued me, I, Mennofar the Goblin, vow that I shall answer one yes-or-no question a day until the third vow is made or until you are dead," said Mennofar. "Whichever comes first."

That brought the boy up short. "Until you are dead" might mean the same thing as "for the rest of your life," but they did not sound the same at all. Specifically, the first sounded like it might happen a lot sooner than the second.

"And as I am feeling generous, you can even save them up from day to day," said Mennofar. "Now, what would you like to know more than anything else?"

The boy considered his first question. There were so many things worth knowing. The most important was how to prove his innocence. The problem with a question like that was that he was not really innocent. He may not have killed Tibor, but he had done nothing to stop it. And he had run away.

The boy pushed from his mind the image of dead Tibor with his eye pointing slackly down. Perhaps buried treasure was the way to go. Of course, how to get there with just yes-or-no questions was not exactly obvious. As he thought about these problems, he rubbed his father's ring between his fingers. The first question was going to be very important. He knew he should think hard and pick it carefully. But he didn't. Instead, he just blurted out, "Am I truly and justly a slave?"

He had no idea where this question came from. In The Tales, people were always discovering secrets about their birth or destiny, but there was usually some clue. There was no reason to believe he wasn't truly a slave. It was a silly thing to ask.

But it was too late. That was his question for the day.

Mennofar nodded. He closed his eyes and looked within for a long moment. As he did, his skin turned an emerald green so brilliant he almost glowed. "A most excellent question," he said, with a smile that exposed his hundreds of pointy teeth. "The answer is no."

6

"I'm not a slave! I'm not a slave!" yelled the boy at the hills. He jumped into the air and danced around in circles and whooped for joy. He threw Mennofar into the air and caught him. Then he hugged the spluttering goblin to his chest.

Mennofar wriggled out of the boy's grasp. "That will be quite enough of that." He dusted himself off.

"But this is wonderful news," said the boy. All his worries disappeared like mist on a summer morning. The Ninety-Nine Duties flew out of his head. He'd never been able to remember more than a dozen at a time, anyway.

The terrible image of dead Tibor lying on the ground vanished. He could even admit, if only to himself, that he had never really liked Tibor. Best of all, the clutching feeling around his heart was gone. He had not defied the will of the gods.

He closed his eyes and pictured the Three Sisters as they sat around their stone bowl. One would draw the boy's stone, keeping it in her closed hand. So that all would know the draw was fair, she would not get the one eye the Sisters all shared until after she had drawn. Then the gnarled old hand would open, and the smooth, worn stone would declare his true fate.

Of course, he had no idea what that fate might be. But once he discovered it, he could tell Casimir. Then he and his former master would be friends. They would have a laugh at the big misunderstanding, whatever it turned out to be.

Unless Casimir had known all along. Then he should be punished. The boy did not know the punishment for falsely enslaving people, but it was probably something horrible like being boiled in vinegar or made to pay a large fine.

But Casimir could not have known. Anyone could see that Casimir was a proper gentleman. Surely he would only buy and sell proper slaves.

"You don't think Casimir knew, do you?" asked the boy. "When the time comes, I'll need to know whether to have him fined."

"I have already answered today's question, impatient one," said Mennofar. "And if you want to punish Casimir, you will need to avoid dying for want of food first."

So the boy tore the left sleeve off his suit and turned it into a slingshot. An afternoon's practice ended with the boy putting stone to target every time. That night's hunt was another matter. Although there were plenty of bats, hitting a moving bat at night was very different from hitting a still target during the day. Shortly before the sun came up, he returned to camp empty-handed and hungry.

"No luck," he told Mennofar.

"I would like to tell you that you are sure to do better tomorrow," said Mennofar.

"Really?" said the boy.

"That is what I would like to tell you," said Mennofar. "But as I have vowed to never lie to you, I cannot."

"I am ready to ask my next question," said the boy. In The Tales, the hero often had to figure out who he really was and then prove it. There was always some clue, like a birthmark or a special object. The boy pulled his father's ring out from under his shirt. "Does this explain who I am?"

Mennofar studied the ring for a moment. Then he closed his eyes and concentrated. After a moment, his skin turned emerald. He smiled and said, "Yes."

The boy looked down at the cracked and bent piece of metal. Once he discovered his fate, the ring would be his proof. And someone had tried to destroy it. Some villain was trying to cheat him of an important fate, a great destiny. The boy knew it was a great destiny because someone had taken it. In The Tales, no one ever went to the trouble of stealing the son of a shepherd or a shopkeeper. When a child was stolen away and sold into slavery, it was always to cheat him of an important birthright.

These schemes never worked out in the end. The child always grew up to be a hero who would have to solve a puzzle and defeat three monsters, each more fearsome than the last, before taking terrible vengeance on the traitor. Only then could he finally return to reclaim his birthright. Now that the boy knew he was such a hero, all he had to do was overcome every obstacle that lay in his path and prove that he was worthy of his birthright. Then he would be restored to the life he was supposed to have, the one the gods had chosen for him.

He still did not thank the Sisters for his fate before he went to sleep. That would have to wait until he discovered what it was.

That night, he dreamed he sat on a throne in his palace, slaves fanning him and bringing him tray after tray of iced cakes. All the beautiful ladies of the court gazed on him adoringly, and all the gentlemen envied him. It was a wonderful dream, but as is often the case with dreams, when he tried to bring the details into focus, they slipped away from him.

♠

It was already midday when he woke. Through the afternoon, he trudged west, carrying Mennofar farther from Nikola and his caravan. He hunted again that evening and had no more luck than the first night. When he returned to camp, he woke Mennofar.

"I am ready to make my first guess," said the boy. "Am I a prince who was stolen away and sold into slavery by a jealous uncle who wished to inherit the throne in my place?"

Mennofar stretched and yawned. "A fine question. A classic taken from The Tales," said Mennofar.

"The Tale of the Magister and the Orphan," said the boy.

Mennofar smiled broadly, exposing his many pointy teeth. "The answer is no."

The boy nodded. He was disappointed, of course, but he could hardly expect to guess the right answer on his first try.

On the third night, he finally managed to bring down a bat. The boy carried his trophy back to camp. As they had no fire, they had to eat it raw. Three days with no food proved sauce enough to let the boy choke it down. Mennofar, the boy could not help noticing, wolfed his share down with gusto.

Once the boy had gotten down as much as he could stand, he lay back and let his unhappy stomach go to work. As he lay there, he thought about what to ask Mennofar next. The Tale of the Magister and the Orphan seemed like the closest fit. The Tale of the Old Woman and the Young Girl had some similarities, but the young girl knew she was a princess. She just couldn't tell anyone because she was under a spell.

The trouble was that Mennofar was so very tricky. Even if the boy got the general story right, Mennofar would latch on to any little difference to answer no. The boy sat up and said, "Mennofar, am I a prince who was stolen away and sold into slavery by a man who had the same father as my father, but a different mother, who would then be my father's half brother instead of his brother, or my half uncle instead of my uncle, so that he, my half uncle, might inherit the throne in my place?"

"Your mind is truly a wonder to behold," said Mennofar. "I mean that metaphorically, of course. I am sure that literally it is gray and spongy like everyone else's." He smiled. "And the answer is no."

The boy's heart sank. He was sure this was going to be the right question. For just a few moments, everything seemed to be falling into place. He had, after all, finally hit a bat. Then he had worked out how Mennofar might have been using a picky, hairsplitting technicality to keep his birthright from him. When he'd thought it up, it had seemed so perfect that it had to be right. Now that he knew it was wrong, the whole task seemed impossible. The boy sighed heavily.

Mennofar patted the boy on the back. "I think you need a little help," said Mennofar.

"You're going to give me a clue?" said the boy.

"Don't be ridiculous," said Mennofar. "I will, however, tell you something helpful. Just this once. Don't go thinking I'll do it again."

"I won't," said the boy.

Mennofar closed his eyes and sat very still. After a long moment, his skin slowly grew brighter until it was a vivid emerald green. Then he said, "It will be very hard to prove you are not a slave. You will almost certainly fail and probably die, but in the unlikely event you do manage it, you will do so in the city of Farnham."

"Where is that?" asked the boy.

"It is in the Kingdom of West Stanhope," said Mennofar, opening his eyes. And as the boy's next question was obvious, he added, "The Kingdom of West Stanhope is very far away, so it is going to be quite a trek. Which is just as well since that will give you time to work on your little puzzle."

In fact, West Stanhope was very, very far away. Some might even have said very, very, *very* far away. It lay along the south side of the Spine, just as High Albemarle did, but it lay as far to the west as High Albemarle did to the east.

For a long time, the boy had to carry Mennofar, and even when Mennofar was well enough to walk on his own, his little legs could not carry him very quickly over the broken ground and hilly country. Nights were spent hunting bats. And even when the boy grew skilled at knocking them out of the sky, every night's hunt cost them a half day's march. The trip was long. It was slow, it was tedious, and he had to sleep in the open on the cold, stony ground.

Along the way, the boy ruled out a great many possibilities. Not only was he not a prince who had been sold into slavery by a jealous uncle or half uncle, but he also had not been sold by a usurping cousin or half cousin. He also ruled out being spirited away by a scheming stepmother who wanted a son of her own on the throne. Then it occurred to him that his story might be more like The Tale of the Colored Coat. When he followed that line, it turned out that he was not stolen away by tinkers. Or travelers. Or elves or sprites or brownies or fey folk or any of a dozen other magical races that stole babies and left changelings behind. And he might not even be a prince. He could be the son of a duke, the heir of a baron or the scion of an earldom stolen by gnomes. To his intense frustration, he found that he could combine the possibilities into dozens, even hundreds, of scenarios.

When they finally came down from the foothills of the Spine, they still had to skirt the northern edge of the Little Dismal and cross some of West Stanhope's dreariest moors. Only then did they finally come to a town.

Exhausted, they snuck into the first barn they saw and bunked down in the haystack for a long rest.

It was the best night's sleep the boy had ever enjoyed, right up until he was stabbed in the arm.

♠

The King ordered all his knights and all his men-at-arms to go after the dragon. This was not so many as Oswald might have hoped for, since the shortage of knights was affecting the royal household as well. The King also decreed that a proclamation be read in each town and village, at every market and inn, and at all the crossroads in the kingdom: whoever rescued the Princess would have any boon within the King's power to grant.

The King assured Oswald that both their daughters would be home soon, but Oswald was not so sure. All the way back to Middlebury, he fretted that Plain Alice would be overlooked in the rush to rescue the Princess. Still, he had done all he could. Knights had ridden out, and a great reward was on offer. The prospect of a sack of gold, a title of nobility or even the hand of a princess was a powerful motivator. He could only hope that it would inspire the right kind of young hero, one who would rescue Plain Alice, too.

It was late in the evening when he finally arrived home. He fell into bed and slept deeply. In the morning, he went out to the barn to feed the animals. First he slopped the pigs. Then he went to fork some hay for Old Bess.

But when he jabbed the pitchfork into the haystack, it yelped in pain and spat forth a shrieking boy. Oswald was startled but not surprised. He found someone bunking down in his haystack a couple of times a year. Usually it was some blacksmith's apprentice who had run away. "Go on, then," said Oswald. He waved the pitchfork at the boy. "Shove off, or I'll stab you."

"You already stabbed me," said the boy. Though the boy had his hand on the wound, it still bled.

"That was an accident. I didn't know you were there," said Oswald. Then, to sound more menacing, he added, "Now go back to your master's hearth, or I'll stab you properly. I'm not getting in trouble for sheltering some renegade apprentice."

"I'm not a renegade apprentice," protested the boy.

Oswald peered a little more closely. The boy's skin was olive brown, and his tangle of hair was black as ink. He also had an accent. He rasped his hard consonants and rolled his *r*'s a bit.

The boy was not from one of the Stanhopes, nor from Clontarf, either. Oswald had met people as dark as this boy, but they all came from lands that were very far away. Then, too, the boy was dressed in the tattered remains of a foreign suit of some quality, one that was much too large for the boy.

There was a story here, of that Oswald was sure, but Oswald was in the middle of a story of his own. He wanted no part of the boy's. "It doesn't matter where you came from," said Oswald. "You'll have to go."

"We'll go. We'll go," said the boy.

Oswald spun to face the haystack. "We? Do you have a girl in there with you?" he said. "Come out, lass, or you'll taste the fork as well."

"That would pain me greatly." A goblin emerged from the haystack. "Permit me to introduce myself. I am Mennofar the Goblin, and this is my traveling companion," said Mennofar.

Oswald goggled. In his circle, Oswald was considered a well-traveled man. He had been to foreign lands and seen a few rare and exotic things in his day. He had never, in all that time, met a man who even claimed to have seen a goblin. Yet here one was. "I am Oswald the Sage, of Middlebury," said Oswald. He kept the pitchfork pointed at the goblin, just in case. "What's your friend's name?" he said, nodding toward the boy.

Mennofar looked over at the boy, and the boy muttered, "Haven't got one."

Oswald glanced at the boy suspiciously. When he did, he saw that the boy's arm was still bleeding freely. "You really did get stuck there, didn't you?" said Oswald.

"I'm fine," said the boy. He turned a little so the injury was facing away from Oswald.

"Don't be ridiculous. You don't want that going foul,"

said Oswald. He set down the pitchfork and went to have a look. The wound was not too serious, but it was narrow and deep, the kind most likely to foul. "This should really be cleaned and dressed. Come to the house, and I'll see to it."

He looked down at the boy. His flesh was thin over his bones. He had not eaten well in some time. Oswald wondered if poor Alice was hungry, too. "And breakfast," he said. "I won't send you away hungry."

"A proper breakfast?" said the boy. "With eggs and bacon and toast and all?"

"Yes, of course," said Oswald. At least, if he had any bacon.

"It has been a while since he has had a meal he actually likes," said Mennofar.

A short while later, Oswald was loading eggs, bacon and toast slathered in butter onto the boy's plate. The boy paused just long enough to thank Oswald and then fell upon it like a wolf. It was his third helping.

"Have you had nothing to eat at all?" asked Oswald.

"We've eaten," said the boy between bites. "Bats, mostly. Rats when we could find them."

"Bats?" said Oswald. He made a face.

"Rest assured, sir, they are quite delicious once one has acquired the taste," said Mennofar.

The boy shrugged. "He likes them," he said.

"But you ate them?" asked Oswald.

"A few hungry days and there's a lot that'll go down," said the boy.

Oswald nodded. "Mennofar, I am told that goblins know all," he said. "My daughter has been kidnapped. Forgive the imposition, but can you tell me where she is?"

"I would be only too pleased to come to the aid of a man of learning," said Mennofar. "Your daughter is—"

"He's a goblin," said the boy. "You can't trust him."

"You wound me, sir," said Mennofar.

"You were about to tell him a huge whopper," said the boy.

"You seem very sure of that claim," said Mennofar.

"You didn't even look through your third eye," said the boy.

"Ah," said Mennofar. "A point I am obliged to concede."

"He'll never tell you the truth," said the boy. "He can't help it. It's his peculiar goblinish sense of honor."

"And there is no way to get the truth from him?" said Oswald.

"He can't lie to me," said the boy. "So if he tells me where she is, you'll know it's true."

They both turned to Mennofar.

"You know that I am under no obligation to say anything at all," said Mennofar.

Oswald looked at him with all the sadness in his heart.

"Fine," said Mennofar through gritted teeth. He

closed his eyes and concentrated. "Oswald has a pretty daughter named Alice, though she is called plain." He concentrated a moment more. His brow wrinkled in confusion and worry. He opened his eyes. "Forgive me my rudeness, O host, but what in the world has happened to your daughter?"

"You couldn't see?" said Oswald.

"No, I can see her heading to the barn. After that, there is only blankness," said Mennofar, "and that happens only when great magical power is involved. Gods or demons or—"

"Or dragons," said Oswald.

"What happened?" asked the boy.

And like that, the dam broke. The whole story poured from Oswald: the death of his wife, his failures as a farmer, his debts, the kidnapping of his daughter and his inability to find anyone who would rescue her. When he was done, he was sobbing freely.

"A tragic tale," said Mennofar, looking at the boy.

"It is," said the boy.

"If only there were someone, some hero, to rescue her," said Mennofar, staring at the boy.

"Yes, do you know any heroes?" asked the boy.

Mennofar glared at him.

"Me?" said the boy in surprise.

"Do you or do you not have a great fate?" asked Mennofar.

The boy put his hand on his father's ring. "I do, but—"

"And in The Tales, do those with important fates not have to defeat a monster to reclaim their birthrights?"

There was a certain logic to what Mennofar said. "Usually it's three, each more terrible than the last," said the boy.

"But to defeat three, you would have to start with one, would you not?" asked Mennofar.

"But it's a dragon," said the boy. Dragons were already pretty terrible. He did not want to think about what would have to come next. "Should I?" he asked.

Mennofar rolled his eyes back up into his head. "You must learn to phrase your questions better," he said. "That is a very difficult question to answer, because—"

"Mennofar," the boy interrupted. "Do *you* think I should rescue her?"

Mennofar smiled. "Why, yes. Yes, I do."

The boy nodded. It made sense. In The Tales, the hero had to prove himself to claim his destiny, and slaying monsters was how birthrights were justified. He swallowed hard. "Oswald the Sage," he said, "on my honor, I swear that I will rescue Alice from the dragon."

7

Though he couldn't say exactly when it happened, the life of Casimir the Merchant took a downward turn at some point. It was only a little turn. His great fortune, nearly enough to make him a notable, was still intact. No catastrophe had befallen him, unless one counted the disappearance of Tibor, which Casimir did not. He had other sons, cleverer ones. Still, an accumulation of little things had begun to drain the joy from life.

Casimir's wife, as it turned out, was very attached to Tibor for some reason. She spent every waking hour wailing and crying over Tibor's disappearance, only stopping long enough to nag Casimir about his fate.

Then his wife's cousin, a loathsome, froggy-looking man, used Tibor's disappearance as an excuse to escape Mossglum, which was, by all accounts, a boggy hole. He ensconced himself in Casimir's home. He said he was there to comfort Casimir's wife. Somehow, this involved encouraging her to carry on howling while he used sweet whispers and cheap jewelry to distract the prettiest serving girls from their duties. This particularly annoyed Casimir. They were *his* prettiest serving girls. They should be distracted from their duties by *him,* not some froggy in-law of his. To escape, Casimir retreated first to the inner and then to the outer courtyard.

Lounging on a divan, he looked over his balance sheets while the Factor hovered nearby. Casimir sighed and wiped the perspiration from his forehead. "Fan harder, curse you," said Casimir to his slave. "Or do you want the flogging of a lifetime?" But it was no use. All the plants in the inner and outer courtyards had shriveled up and died quite suddenly, though why they should do so was a complete mystery. The courtyards went from being cool, shady refuges to baking stone pits. Even his favorite fanning slave could not keep him cool.

Casimir tossed the balance sheets aside. "I cannot think in this heat," he said. "Just tell me what it all means."

"Your businesses are all doing well," said the Factor.

"Trade is up, and you are making good money on your ventures."

"Not on all of them, surely," said Casimir. There were too many for that. "There must be one, somewhere, that needs my attention."

"At the moment, no," said the Factor. "I am pleased to report successes across the board."

"That is totally unacceptable," said Casimir.

"Umm," said the Factor. "Er . . ." Then he tried, "Sorry?"

"A man must have something to do," said Casimir. "I must have a reason to leave this house." And to escape his wailing wife and her froggy cousin.

"I deeply regret these successes," said the Factor. "I take full responsibility for them."

Casimir scowled at the Factor. It was no use. A pinchface like the Factor could never understand the problems of a man of the world. Casimir sat up and said, "Bring me the latest reports from my foreign agents."

The Factor went pale, but that was no surprise. The man hated to travel.

"At once!" said Casimir. The Factor rose and shuffled off, grumbling the whole time. Casimir smiled. Sea air and new sights would do much to refresh Casimir's weary mind. A trading expedition to some new port was just the thing.

♠

There was a long silence as the boy, Mennofar and Oswald thought about the gravity of what the boy had done. Finally, Oswald said, "Lad, that's very generous, but you can't possibly—"

"Are you saying I have no honor?" said the boy.

Oswald jumped back a little. "No, no, I'm sorry. It's not that," he said. "I'm sure you're very honorable. I meant only, um, that you have no arms or armor, I suppose?"

"I should," said the boy. "Maybe you have some I can borrow?"

"Me? No, I've got nothing. I'm a sage, not a soldier," said Oswald. He stroked his beard for a moment. "Well, I do have this knife." He got down his biggest kitchen knife. It wasn't much to look at. It had a rough wooden handle, and the blade had turned reddish brown with rust. Still, it held a keen edge, and Oswald had recently had it sharpened. He set it on the table in front of the boy.

Sturdy as it was, it did not look adequate for dragon slaying. Oswald looked up at the boy and saw the bandage. "The pitchfork." He dashed outside and brought it in from the barn.

He was about to sit down again when he realized that there was one more thing he could give the boy. He fetched Magan from his bedroom and set her on the table in front of the boy. Mennofar and the boy leaned forward to look at the shield. "She's called Magan," said Oswald. The Earl would be mightily displeased when he found out, but that didn't matter as much as Alice.

The boy nodded and accepted the shield.

In addition to arming the boy, Oswald packed a large sack with all of the sausage, cheese and bread he had in the house. He fetched his waterskin and filled it from the well. The boy wrapped the kitchen knife in a cloth and stuck it in his belt. For good measure, he tucked his slingshot into his belt as well. He and Oswald cobbled together a strap for the pitchfork out of some old pieces of rope. The waterskin went over one of the boy's shoulders and the bag of food over the other. Then he slung the pitchfork over his back as well. Over all of this, he put Magan, which he could only barely fit on, even with the traveling straps loosened all the way.

When the boy was ready to go, Oswald embraced him. "Thank you again, son," said Oswald. "Your courage shames me." He began to mist up.

The boy looked away down the road. "Well," he said. "Well, I'd best be on my way. . . ." He glanced down the road in the other direction. "Wait, where am I going?" he asked, and turned to Mennofar.

Mennofar sighed heavily. "As I cannot see dragons," he said, "I do not know where they abide."

"Yes, of course," said the boy.

To Oswald, Mennofar said, "Where does this road go?"

"This is the Stanhope Road," said Oswald. "It runs from Farnham, in the west, to Uskborough, the capital of

East Stanhope. That's in the east. Obviously." He pointed in each direction as he spoke.

"What is between here and Farnham?" asked Mennofar.

"It's some very nice farm country with several lovely villages along the way," said Oswald. "Nothing fancy, mind you, but good, solid people all."

"And the other way?" asked Mennofar.

"There are a few farms that way, too, for a bit, until you get to the castle of Duke Geoffrey. After that, there's the Little Dismal, then the Mountains of Fire, and if you go through the mountains over the Traitor's Pass, there's the Great Dismal. If you survive all that, you're in East Stanhope," said Oswald.

"Great Dismals, Mountains of Fire, Traitor's Passes—it all sounds like dragon country to me," said Mennofar.

"Me too," said the boy.

And so they went east.

Oswald watched them go. Though the boy was almost a young man, he looked very small under his load of equipment. Oswald told himself it would be all right. In The Tales, dragons were always slain by unlikely heroes. The trouble was that The Tales were a load of old nonsense. Everyone knew that.

♠

The farther east Mennofar and the boy went, the less fertile the land around them became. The farms grew poorer and farther apart. Slowly, the countryside sank into an empty, stony, gray waste. It was gloomy country, but Mennofar and the boy had spent many weeks traveling along the Spine, which was even emptier and stonier and grayer. Instead of cursing the bleak landscape, they appreciated having a good road. They made much better time than they had over the broken ground of the Spine.

Toward the end of the day, they came to a huge black stone fortress. It squatted on a low hill, from which it commanded the flat, open country for miles around. It was a strange and lonely spot for a castle.

Mennofar pointed to the pennant flying from the highest tower. "Those are the colors of West Stanhope they are flying. Perhaps they will put us up for the night," he said.

The boy nodded in agreement. Though the castle looked foreboding, the colors they flew should mean that its inhabitants were friendly. Mennofar and the boy approached the castle bar. A bored guardsman stood watch. In the courtyard, a group of small boys threw pebbles at an unhappy cat. "Halt. What business have you with my master, Duke Geoffrey?" said the guardsman. His tone suggested that he said this dozens of times a day, though Mennofar and the boy had seen no one on the road at all.

"We are travelers, seeking only shelter for the night," said the boy.

"What business have you with my master, Duke Geoffrey?" said the guard in the same bored tone.

"We have no business with the Duke," said the boy. "We were just looking for—"

"The Duke's a very busy and important man, and he cannot be disturbed," said the guard.

"We'll have to look elsewhere," said the boy to Mennofar, and he turned to leave.

When the boy began to turn away from him, the guard snapped out of his rut. "Oy," he said, pointing to Magan. "Them's the colors of the Earl of Middlebury."

The boy glanced at Mennofar, who nodded. "That's right," he said.

"You his champion or something, then?" said the guard.

"Um," said the boy. Mennofar was still nodding. "Yes, of course, how could there be any doubt?"

"Why go keeping that a secret?" said the guard. He called out to the nearest pebble thrower. "Go and tell the Majordomo the Earl of Middlebury's champion is here." The pebble thrower wrinkled his nose and stuck out his tongue at the guard. "I'll box your ears and tip you headfirst into the privy if you don't," said the guard, raising his hand and taking a few steps forward. That was enough to send the pebble thrower off at a run. "It'll be a few minutes," said the guard.

While they waited, the boy whispered to Mennofar, "He didn't seem to notice that you're a goblin."

"That happens a lot," said Mennofar. "People see what they expect to see."

The Majordomo turned out to be a thin, balding man with the kind of lines on his face that come from perpetually scowling. He rubbed his hands together in excitement. He bowed deeply and said, "Good afternoon, good afternoon, good sir." Then he actually looked at the boy. "You're the Earl's champion?"

"Yes, sir," said the boy.

"But you're—" The Majordomo stopped himself. "Follow me, please." The boy and Mennofar followed the Majordomo through the gate, across the courtyard and into the antechamber of the receiving hall. "Wait here. The Duke will see you in a few minutes." Then he slipped between the doors into the receiving hall. In the brief moment the doors were open, the boy could hear people laughing.

They sat and waited. And waited. And waited. After several hours, the boy said, "Do you think they've forgotten us?"

"If they have, we can always spend the night on these benches," said Mennofar. "It will still be better than sleeping on the ground by the road."

No sooner had Mennofar said this than the doors of the receiving hall flew open.

♠

The champion had to be received. He was the representative of an earl, after all, but Geoffrey was a duke. Protocol might require him to put a champion up for the night, but he could still insult the man. Or he could if the insult was clever, twisty and backhanded enough that he could pretend he had not meant it that way. And he intended to do exactly that, if only to remind everyone that a duke outranks even an earl.

When the Majordomo led him out into the antechamber, however, he did not see the champion. There was just a grubby boy dressed in rags. "May the Foul One take your hide. I've told you to just turn the beggars away," snapped Duke Geoffrey.

"Ah, sir, this boy is not just a beggar," said the Majordomo. "He is also the champion of the Earl of Middlebury."

"How extraordinary," said Duke Geoffrey. He looked down his nose at the boy. "What's your name, boy?"

The boy fell on all fours and pressed his forehead to the floor. "Haven't got one, uh—"

"Your Grace," whispered the Majordomo.

"Haven't got one, Your Grace," said the boy.

"The Earl picked a nameless, grubby ragamuffin for his champion?" said the Duke.

"Perhaps he was impressed by the boy's trained monkey, Your Grace," said the Majordomo. Duke Geoffrey vaguely recalled that monkeys were covered in fur, and he was confident they did not turn a poisonous shade of dark green when insulted.

"At least he knows how to bow properly," said Duke Geoffrey. "So few do nowadays." He turned back to the boy. "And what errand has he set for you, O nameless champion?"

"To rescue the girl Alice from the clutches of the dragon, Your Grace," said the boy.

Duke Geoffrey choked a little. Princess Alice was of royal blood. Kidnapping her was one thing, but allowing a jumped-up guttersnipe to refer to her as simply "the girl" was flatly unacceptable. Ordinarily, he would have just had the boy hanged and been done with the matter. But Duke Geoffrey's plans were under way. It was no time to pick a quarrel with the Earl of Middlebury. Besides, Duke Geoffrey could always hang the boy later, once he was king. Instead, he took a deep breath and counted to ten, just as his mother had taught him. "Mind that tongue," he said. "You may have gained the favor of an earl, but that's no excuse to be pert to your betters."

"Yes, Your Grace, sorry, Your Grace," said the boy, though he looked confused.

"Well, I'm afraid I'll be dining privately tonight," said Duke Geoffrey. It was a deliberate insult, but for some reason, the boy did not react at all. Annoyed, Duke Geoffrey turned to the Majordomo. "Find them somewhere to stay for the night and get them some food."

"Yes, Your Grace," said the Majordomo, scurrying out a side door.

♠

When the Duke stormed out, the boy noticed something odd. On the back of his neck, the Duke had a small tattoo like a spade from a playing card. In High Albemarle, only thieves, murderers and Rotarians got tattoos. Of course, tattoos might be more respectable in West Stanhope. Or dukes less.

The Majordomo returned and led the boy and Mennofar out to a little shack next to the stables. He threw open the door with a flourish and said, "Here we are, nice and cozy." The shack was almost entirely filled by two rough cots made of woven rope. The Majordomo waited for an objection but got none. "Ah! And here's your dinner," he said as a serving girl arrived with cold meat, bread and water.

"It looks wonderful," said the boy.

The Majordomo scowled and slunk out.

"What's eating him?" said the boy.

"You were supposed to expect better hospitality, I suspect," said Mennofar. "They have been trying to insult you."

In Casimir's villa, the boy had slept under the eaves of the stable on a reed mat. He had never slept indoors, and certainly not on a bed, before. "If this is bad hospitality, I'm almost afraid to see the good."

The next morning, the boy's arm was tender and sore. There was nothing to be done about it, but the boy went ahead and poked at it until it really hurt anyway. Neither he nor Mennofar wanted to see the Duke or the Major-domo again, so they simply left without saying anything to anyone. They walked all day. East of Castle Geoffrey, the air slowly grew damper and the land soggier. The undernourished gray-brown grass became greener and deeper. The scrubby little brush grew larger and heavier until it formed great thickets. When these thickets were overtaken by gnarled, fat-bottomed trees wallowing in the soupy mud and garlanded with mosses, they knew they had arrived in the Little Dismal.

Mosquitoes began torturing them as soon as the sun went low, but the stinging ants were thoughtful enough to wait until they made camp. They slept on the road itself, as the packed earth was the only solid ground to be found. Even though the swamp surrounding them was alive with small animals, the boy did not try to hunt. They ate only hard bread and cheese. The boy barely picked at this helping, for he felt feverish and out of sorts.

"I've been thinking about my question for the day,"

said the boy. "What if Casimir did know? Suppose he had a reason for falsely enslaving me."

"Interesting," said Mennofar. "What did you have in mind?"

"Like Casimir, my father is a rich and powerful merchant," said the boy. "They have some dealings together, and Casimir becomes convinced that my father has cheated him in some way." He put his palms out. "It's all in his head, of course, because my father would be perfectly honest."

"Naturally," said Mennofar.

"So Casimir has me stolen away and brought up a slave in revenge," said the boy.

"You took that from The Tale of the Two Knights?" said Mennofar.

"The Tale of the Tortoise's Reprieve," said the boy. "Casimir would be the water buffalo, and my father would be the tortoise—or, no, I would. Something like that. Anyway, is that what happened?"

"No," said Mennofar.

That night, the boy's dreams were filled with wild visions of tortoises locked in mortal combat with knights, and dragons suing water buffaloes in court. The boy slept until midmorning, and only woke then because Mennofar roused him.

"Are you well?" asked Mennofar.

"I don't feel very good," said the boy. Despite his

long, solid night of sleep, he was tired and achy. During the night, his arm had swollen and turned red. It was very tender to the touch.

"Your wound is making you ill," said Mennofar. "Miserable though this place is, we should camp here for another day or two while you get better."

"We can't do that," said the boy. "Poor Alice has been the dragon's prisoner for over a week."

"You cannot slay a dragon when you are ill," said Mennofar.

"Can I slay one when I'm well?" asked the boy.

Mennofar considered the question for a moment. "Probably not," he admitted. "But we do not even know where we are going."

"Isn't there anything you can do about that?" asked the boy.

Mennofar said, "Gods, demons and—"

"And dragons, I remember, but we're not trying to find out anything about the dragon. We're trying to find out something about the *girl.* What if you ignored the dragon and just concentrated on the girl?" said the boy.

"I do not think that would work," said Mennofar. "All such beings cast a shadow. I cannot see anything directly associated with them."

"Please try," said the boy.

The boy clutched himself and tried to look as pathetic as he could. Mennofar sighed, closed his eyes and concentrated. He promptly turned bright green.

"You've found her," said the boy. "So my idea worked?"

"Not even slightly," said Mennofar. "However, it happens that she is no longer being held prisoner by the dragon but by an ogre."

The boy sat up a little. "An ogre?" he said. "So she needs rescuing from something—"

"More slayable?" said Mennofar.

"Where is she?" the boy wanted to know.

"He has her locked up a few miles from here."

"A few miles from here? Let's go." The boy jumped to his feet, which made him so dizzy he staggered.

"Please reconsider," said Mennofar. "You are genuinely ill. You need to rest and recuperate."

"No, I need to rescue that poor girl," said the boy. "I gave my word of honor that I would."

Mennofar said, "Yes, well, of course, but—"

"I've never given my word of honor before," shouted the boy. Then, more quietly, he said, "I never knew I could. How would it be if I failed because I did less than my utmost?" He took a few steps but wobbled a bit. "Just how much danger is she in?"

"Quite a lot, I am afraid," said Mennofar. "Ogres do enjoy feasting on the flesh of young maidens."

"But he hasn't killed her yet. What're the chances that he will soon?" said the boy.

Mennofar closed his eyes and concentrated. He darkened to an inky tone.

"We have to go now," said the boy.

Mennofar nodded, and began to cache their store of food. The boy tried to lift Magan with his left arm, but the infection had robbed the limb of most of its strength. It was so swollen that he could barely bend his elbow or make a fist. The fingers were hopeless. He could not keep the shield on his arm. "Can't you help me with this?" asked the boy.

"Perhaps if you tied it on?" said Mennofar. He brought the pitchfork and the knife to the boy. Then he tore a few strips from the cloth used to wrap the knife.

The boy used his right arm to wrestle Magan onto his left. He tied Magan's straps to his arm. When he was done, he stood up and promptly toppled over.

Lying flat on his back, he said, "All right, which way?"

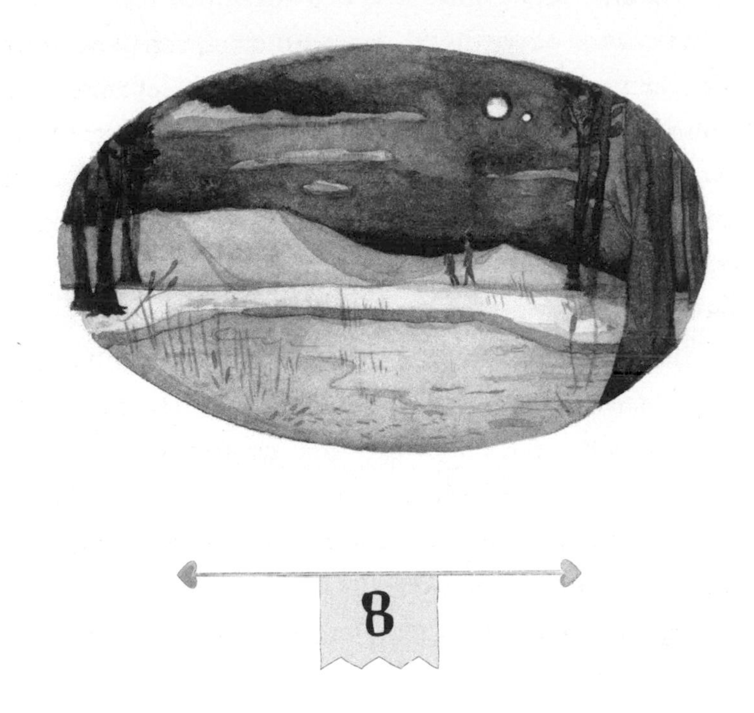

8

Some swamps are great muddy plains. Others are vast soupy bowls, very nearly lakes. The Little Dismal was a bit of both. As soon as the boy stepped off the road, the warm mud oozed up between his toes. Soon he was squelching through mud that came halfway to his knees. It was worse for Mennofar, who sank in up to his waist. Although they found firmer footing not long after, there was nothing reliable in any of the ground they crossed. Semi-solid earth would give way unexpectedly to dark, oily pools, and Mennofar had to ride on the boy's shoulders to cross. From this perch, he would fuss about the rank waters seeping into the boy's wound, but nothing could be done about it. At other times, the cypress trees gave way to great walls of thatch and brush. The boy had to shove his way through the wild tangle with Magan. Between the boy's illness and the terrain, their progress was painfully slow. They spent hours crossing just a few miles. Finally, in the midst of a particularly snarled and thickety patch of brush, Mennofar whispered, "We are here."

The boy looked back at Mennofar. "There's nothing here," he said, pushing forward.

Mennofar said, "Perhaps the element of surprise would—" Only he spoke just a moment too late. For as he spoke, the boy burst out into the ogre's clearing. There he saw the same little wooden hut Plain Alice had seen a few days earlier. The ogre himself lazed on the ground nearby.

The ogre jumped up and roared.

The boy felt his guts go soft and loose. The ogre might have been smaller than a dragon, but he was still twice the boy's height, six times his weight and plainly much, much stronger.

"Foul One take me," said the boy. He gave his father's ring a quick rub for luck.

"You not pretty girl," said the ogre. "Who you?"

"Who's there?" came a girl's voice from inside the hut—it had to be Plain Alice. At least he was not too late.

"I am here to rescue Plain Alice of Middlebury," said the boy as loftily as he could manage.

"Alice? Who Alice?" said the ogre.

"I'm Alice, you dunderhead," said Plain Alice from inside the hut.

"You want pretty girl?" said the ogre. "We fight."

"Yes, we will fight," said the boy. Then he half sat and half fell back onto a log at the edge of the clearing. Sweat poured off of him. He burned with fever and shivered with chill at the same time. "But first, we rest for a few minutes."

This confused the ogre, though confusion was familiar enough that it did not bother him too much. "Rest?" he said. "Why we rest?"

To distract him, the boy said, "Why do you like pretty girls so much?"

The ogre squinted at the boy. "Pretty girls taste good," he said in a tone that suggested it was a silly question.

The boy needed more time to gather his strength. "Um, if they taste so good, well, um, why haven't you eaten her already?" he asked.

"Not ready yet," said the ogre. "Girls taste best when they are green and stinky."

"Green? Stinky? When are they green and stinky?"

"After a few days," said the ogre, just as though the boy had asked him why the sun was yellow.

The boy shook his head to clear his mind. "What are you talking about?"

"I believe he is referring to putrefaction," said

Mennofar, who had stepped out of the brush. To the ogre, he said, "Do you mean a few days after she is dead?"

"Yes," said the ogre. "A few days dead, then yum, yum, yum."

The boy's already queasy stomach somersaulted at the thought, but he managed not to retch. "But she's not dead," said the boy.

The ogre's tiny eyes narrowed. His face was a portrait of brainless incomprehension.

"Did you forget to kill her?" asked Mennofar.

Slowly, understanding dawned on the ogre's face. "I forgets to kill her," he howled. He turned to rush toward the hut.

The opportunity was clear, even through the feverish haze that clouded the boy's mind. As the ogre turned away from him, the boy gathered the last of his strength. He sprang up and launched himself at the ogre, throwing the full force of his weight behind the pitchfork. He slammed it into the ogre's back.

The pitchfork bit deep into the ogre's flesh, but not deep enough to penetrate the thick layers of fat and muscle that protected the ogre's vitals. The boy injured the ogre, but not nearly as gravely as he needed to.

The ogre roared in surprise. And pain. And rage. He spun to face the boy. The boy hunkered down behind Magan and waved the pitchfork at the ogre to keep him at bay. The ogre batted the pitchfork aside, launching it ten yards from the boy's hands. He tried to knock Magan aside, too, but it was too firmly tied to the boy's arm. He wound up twisting the boy's arm savagely.

Pain shot through the boy's shoulder. His eyes filled with tears. He didn't see the ogre coming, and the next thing he knew, his opponent had a great meaty paw around one of his ankles. The ogre spun the boy around in the air. The boy's stomach flopped and churned. Too well anchored to fly off, Magan whipped back and forth. His arm shrieked in agony, blood thundered to his head and he teetered on the edge of blacking out.

"The knife!" said Mennofar. "The knife!"

The boy bit down hard against the panic. He drew the knife from his belt. The ogre pulled him close and began to lift him in the air. Even hanging upside down, the boy managed to cut the ogre's flank on his way up, though with little force. He only barely opened the skin. The ogre did not even notice. The boy had a weapon but no way to use it.

The ogre swung the boy high into the air. The boy saw what was coming next. The ogre was going to dash his head open on the ground. He had just one chance. He stuck the knife out as far as he could. When the ogre brought him down with full force, he plunged the knife into the ogre's foot.

The ogre's foot was thick and horny, but the point of the knife struck with all the power the ogre intended for the boy's head. The blade sank hilt-deep in the ogre's foot, slicing through muscle and snapping bone. The tip of the knife broke through the bottom of the ogre's foot. The ogre shrieked in pain.

Of course, the boy could have easily had his brains dashed out anyway. But when the ogre fell back in pain and surprise, he let the boy go. The boy had just enough time to bring Magan up so that the force of his landing was taken up by her broad surface, rather than the narrow crown of his head. The landing dealt another fearsome blow to his poor battered arm. The pain swallowed him up, and he blacked out.

When he came to a few seconds later, he rolled over with Magan on top of him to protect himself. He watched as the ogre stood up on his good foot and took one step forward. For a terrifying instant, the ogre loomed over him. But when the ogre put his full weight on his bad foot, it failed him completely. He howled in pain and came crashing down again. The boy had only a moment. Though his head was swimming, he stood and ran to the hut. He threw the bar and flung the door wide open. "Run," he said.

♠

Plain Alice could not see any of the battle. She tried peering through the cracks, but none of them were wide enough. She did, however, hear all that happened. She cheered when the ogre cried out in pain and was pleased that her rescuer did nothing more than grunt. She thought he might be a seasoned knight or perhaps a canny woodsman, so she was well surprised when the door of the hut flew open to reveal a boy caked with swamp mud. Still, when he managed to rasp out, "Run," she did.

She burst out into the clearing. The ogre lay in the middle, nursing a nasty wound to his foot. On the far side of the clearing, there was, still more improbably, a goblin, waving frantically at her. "This way," he called out.

To avoid the ogre, Plain Alice and the boy skirted the clearing and ran toward the goblin. As they approached, he bowed quickly and said, "Good afternoon, Miss Alice. I am Mennofar the Goblin. Your father dispatched the boy and me to rescue you." Then he started running, too.

"My father?" said Alice. "How did my father—"

"Obviously, that is quite a story," said Mennofar. "But I think we should save it for when we make it to safety."

The ogre rose up on his one good foot and started after them. But as soon as his weight shifted to his bad foot, he went down again with a roar of pain. As they fled into the underbrush, he tried to give chase, first by hopping and then by crawling after them, but his progress was so slow that they quickly left him behind.

After hours of crawling through underbrush, squelching through mud patches and fording pools of slimy water, they popped out of the trees and onto the Stanhope Road. Plain Alice took two steps toward Middlebury but saw that Mennofar and the boy had both stopped.

Mennofar's eyes were closed, and he was concentrating carefully. After a moment, he opened them and said, "We must go the other way, to the east."

"But Middlebury is this way," she said, pointing west.

"Yes, but the nearest sweet water is to the east, and he cannot go much farther," said Mennofar.

By the look of the boy, Mennofar was right. His eyes were glassy and unfocused. His face was red with fever. Sweat poured off of him, streaking the swamp mud caked all over his body. His arm was so swollen that the straps that held the shield bit into his flesh.

Plain Alice nodded. She untied the shield from his arm. When she knocked the worst of the mud from it, the familiar griffin crest appeared. "Is this Magan?" she said. "How did he— Never mind. Time enough for the story later."

She slung Magan across her back and they went east. When they got to the cache of food that Mennofar and the boy had left behind that morning, they made themselves a meal of cold sausage, bread and cheese. The boy ate little. After so many days without food, Plain Alice ate slowly and with great care. Even so, she felt slightly sick. For his part, Mennofar wolfed down his meal. When he was done, he told her how the two of them had come to meet her father and everything that had happened since.

"You took a vow to rescue me when we had never even met. That was brave," said Plain Alice to the boy. "A little stupid, maybe, but brave."

The boy only grunted in response.

"We should get going," said Mennofar.

"Is that such a good idea?" said Plain Alice. "I mean, look at him. He can barely move."

"Yes, but we'll need good water if he's to recover," said Mennofar. "And it's not far."

And so they pressed on. Mennofar led the way while Plain Alice steered the boy in the right direction. When they came to the spot where the road broke out of the Little Dismal and began to rise into the Mountains of Fire, Mennofar showed her where there was a hidden spring just south of the road. There they all flopped to the ground and slept heavily through the night.

In the morning, Plain Alice and Mennofar woke early while the boy slept on. Plain Alice washed herself in the spring. While the two of them ate breakfast, she asked Mennofar, "You only ever call him 'the boy.' What's his name?"

"It is complicated," said Mennofar.

"His name?" said Plain Alice. "How can a name be complicated?"

"It is his story to tell," said Mennofar. "Or not tell."

Plain Alice went to check up on the boy and discovered that he was in the throes of a very high fever. He would not wake, so she peeled off his shirt. It was just as well that the shirt was missing one sleeve, for the boy's injured arm had swollen to twice its normal size. Although there were some nasty bruises from when the boy had braced himself with Magan, the real worry was the punctures from the pitchfork. They were dark purple, wept pus and smelled terrible. She pointed them out to Mennofar.

"They were already foul yesterday," said Mennofar. "Mucking around in filthy swamp water cannot have helped."

"We have to watch him," said Plain Alice. "If his fingers turn black, we'll have to take his arm to save his life."

In the meantime, she tore a strip of cloth from the hem of her dress, washed it in the spring and made it into a cold compress to try to keep his temperature down. She put Mennofar in charge of the compress. She washed the boy's shirt as best she could. Then she used it to clean out his wounds. When that was done, she used the shirt to wash off the rest of him.

Once the mud and dirt came off him, she could see what he really looked like. Stanhopers rarely had hair much darker than dark brown. The boy's was black and fell in loose curls. And Stanhopers were fair-skinned, while the boy was swarthy, swarthier than anyone Plain Alice had ever seen. He was not just a foreigner; he had to come from far away indeed. "Where is he from?" she asked.

"High Albemarle," said Mennofar.

"High Albemarle? That's the far end of the world," said Plain Alice.

"That is putting it strongly," said Mennofar. "It is some way off, though."

"Well, how did you wind up in West Stanhope?" she asked.

Mennofar told her of their time traveling along the Spine. He said nothing of the boy's tale before that.

"It must have taken you ages to get to West Stanhope," said Plain Alice. "Why come all that way?"

"He has an errand in West Stanhope," said Mennofar.

"An errand?" said Plain Alice. "You traveled all that way to run an errand?"

"It is his story, not mine," said Mennofar.

There was clearly more to the story, but it was just as clear that Mennofar was not going to say more.

They took turns cooling the boy with fresh compresses and cleaning his injury when more pus came from it. His fever raged for three days. Then, on the third evening in camp, it broke.

9

The God of War is always attended by his fire maidens, beautiful angels with flames for hair. When a fierce warrior lies wounded or sick, the God of War may show him favor by sending a fire maiden to nurse him back to health. As the boy lay there shivering and sweating, he saw one watching over him and caring for him. His mind, admittedly somewhat addled by fever, accepted this as his due. He had been gravely wounded in battle with a mighty opponent. Surely he had earned the ministrations of a fire maiden. But he hadn't expected her to still be there when he awoke. He reached out toward

Plain Alice's fiery red hair and murmured, "An angel. A beautiful angel."

Plain Alice jumped back a bit. She was not used to hearing soft words from boys. She had an air about her that discouraged them from coming closer than stone-throwing distance. She blushed. "Oh, I, er, um . . . you're awake," she said.

The boy blinked a few times, and his eyes began to focus on her. "Oh, I didn't mean you," he said.

"Well, I'm glad to see you're feeling better," she said.

"No, I just meant that you aren't literally an angel," he said. "I dreamed I was being watched over by a beautiful fire maiden, but now I see it was you."

"Oh, I see," she said, blushing once more.

"But that was just the fever, obviously," said the boy.

She scowled at him. If only he could get himself to shut up. Perhaps the fever had cooked his brain. He tried to raise himself on his elbows, but pain lanced through his bad arm. He cried out and fell back again.

His cry drew Mennofar. "Fever broken, has it?" he said.

"My arm, it hurts bad," said the boy. He wished he didn't sound so whiny in front of Plain Alice.

"You're a lot better, but you'll need a sling," she said. She took the boy's shirt and tore it carefully along the seams. Tying it artfully, she made the pieces into a sling. Amidst cries of pain, tears and curses, she and Mennofar levered the boy's arm into it.

Once he had his arm in the sling, the boy managed to pull himself up enough to sit against a rock. Plain Alice was smiling at him, but the boy didn't like it. It was the kind of smile people gave to small children. Of course, he must have looked like one to her: dirty, bedraggled, dressed in rags. He should look like a hero from The Tales, not a dirty beggar boy.

"I'm sorry, I never did get your name," she said.

The boy looked down. "I haven't got one," he said.

"One what?" said Plain Alice.

"A name," said the boy.

"Don't be ridiculous," she said. "Everyone has a name."

"I don't," said the boy. His face flushed. All she had to do was ask about his name, and suddenly not having one seemed horrible and freakish, like not having a face. Tears stung his eyes.

"But they call you something," said Plain Alice. "What do they call you?"

"Boy," said the boy. "That's not a name, is it?"

"No, it isn't," she said. "I'm sorry. I didn't know that could happen. Or not happen, I suppose. Or— Look, why didn't your parents give you one? Or don't you have any?"

"Course I got parents," mumbled the boy. "Probably." At that very moment, they were sitting in their castle, desperate for their son to return. Or they should be.

"Probably?" said Plain Alice.

"I don't know how to find them," said the boy. "Or who they are."

She knew she should not ask. She was sure he would not want to answer. Still, she said, "But how can you not know—"

"What is with you?" said the boy. "You pick on me, you laugh at me and you make me feel bad. What did I ever do to you? Other than kill an ogre to save you."

"Kill?" said Plain Alice. "Maybe defeat." Then, to the boy's surprise, she added, "It doesn't matter. You're right, of course. You were very brave. A little stupid, perhaps, but still very brave." She leaned over and kissed him on the cheek. "Thank you."

"Oh, um, er, um . . ." The boy's face grew hot, and his thoughts went in every direction at once. Finally, he managed to mumble, "Uh, it was nothing."

Mennofar said, "If you two are finished doing—"

"We weren't doing anything!" said the boy, a little too loudly.

"Then, if the two of you are finished doing nothing," said Mennofar, "we could escort the young lady home."

♠

"I have it," said Casimir. He held the report in the air. "The city of Farnham in West Stanhope."

The Factor consulted the atlas. "'City' seems an

optimistic word for the place," he said. "And it is some distance away."

"Hang the distance," said Casimir. "See what our man in Roggenheim says about the place." He waved the report at the Factor.

The Factor took the sheet of paper and read it. He glanced at the back, but it was blank. "He says that nearby merchants do not bother to travel there."

"Yes, but don't you see what that means?" said Casimir.

"It means that those who know best believe the place is not worth bothering about," said the Factor.

"No, it means there's an opportunity. What if they have piles of gold just waiting to be spent?" said Casimir. "Or what if they have mastered some unknown art? For all we know, they're producing goods that can be found nowhere else in the world!"

"For all we know, it's a jumped-up village of illiterate swineherds," said the Factor.

"It'll be an adventure," said Casimir.

"It'll be bad food and worse wine, none of which will we be able to keep down because of the seasickness," said the Factor. "If we don't drown, we'll be killed by pirates, or even our own crew. And don't forget—"

"This is my absolute wish," said Casimir, and he stamped his foot on the ground.

The Factor slumped a little. "I shall see to the arrangements, sir."

"Your problem is that you lack any sense of adventure," said Casimir. "It's a sad thing to see a man who cannot stand a little discomfort." He shook his head at the small-mindedness of the Factor. Then he turned to his fanning slave. "Curse you, I told you to fan harder."

The fanning slave, already drenched with sweat, redoubled his efforts.

♠

Though his fever had broken, the boy had not recovered fully. Crossing the broken ground back to the Stanhope Road was slow going, and even when they turned onto the road, the boy stumbled more than once.

Finally, Plain Alice stopped and shifted Magan's traveling straps. She was carrying Magan because the boy still wasn't strong enough. "Would you like to rest a bit?"

"I'm fine," said the boy.

"There's nothing to be embarrassed about," said Plain Alice. "You were very sick."

The boy had not been embarrassed until she said he should not be. As soon as she did, the blood rushed to his face. "I want to push on," said the boy. "If we take too long, we'll have to stay at Castle Geoffrey. I don't think the Duke'll be any nicer the second time."

"I shouldn't worry about that," said Plain Alice. "He's sure to be off trying to rescue Princess Alice from the dragon. Every knight and nobleman for five kingdoms will be trying for that honor."

"I still want to make some ground," said the boy.

"Just don't wear yourself out and make yourself sick again," said Plain Alice.

"I can take care of myself," said the boy.

They marched without speaking for a while. Something tickled at the back of the boy's mind. He wanted to talk to Plain Alice, but he had no idea what to talk to her about. Part of the problem was that he could not tell her anything about himself without revealing his secret. That would be a foolish thing to do, until he had his proof. He trusted her, of course, but people made mistakes. The more people who knew, the greater the danger of getting caught. Life in Casimir's villa had taught him that lesson more than once. That was not the only reason, though. He just didn't want her to know. It was as if there were something shameful about having been a slave, though that made no sense. A person's fate was a person's fate. There was no shame in that. Indeed, it was the height of honor to graciously submit to one's fate. Only that could not be quite right because slaves were not supposed to have any honor. Or shame.

It was all very confusing.

And it didn't help that Plain Alice was walking right next to him, and he could not stop wondering what would happen if he tried holding her hand. Confusing indeed.

Mennofar, for his part, had turned a particularly vibrant shade of green. "What're you so happy about?" said the boy, but he saw the answer as soon as he spoke. "Oh. No." The boy turned to Plain Alice. "Did you say 'rescue Princess Alice from the dragon'?"

"Yes, that's who the dragon—his name is Ludwig, by the way—wanted all along," said Plain Alice. "He only kidnapped me by mistake."

"But when did the dragon—Ludwig—kidnap her?" said the boy.

"At least a week ago," said Plain Alice.

"I'm doomed, aren't I?" said the boy.

"Technically, I am supposed to say that I do not actually know," said Mennofar, "but I think it is a safe assumption."

"What's wrong?" said Plain Alice.

"I swore, on my honor, to rescue Alice from the dragon."

"And you did," said Plain Alice. "Well, you rescued me from the ogre because I didn't need to be rescued from the dragon."

"When he took that oath, the Alice being held by the dragon was the Princess, not you," said Mennofar.

"I don't see why you have to be so happy about it," said the boy. "You don't want me to be killed, do you?"

"Is that one of your questions?" said Mennofar. "Should I answer?"

The boy hesitated. If he was killed, Mennofar would be freed from his vows. "No," he said.

Mennofar smiled even more broadly. "Good choice," he said.

"And I definitely swore on my honor?" said the boy.

Mennofar nodded.

"That's how I remembered it, too," said the boy. "I guess I have to do it."

"You can't," said Plain Alice. "You don't understand. He's too powerful." She burst into tears. "It's not fair. I never really had a friend before." Somehow, telling everyone how clever she was had never really endeared her to the boys and girls of the town. "And now that I've found one, he has to run off and get killed by a dragon."

"We're friends?" asked the boy.

"Of course we are, stupid," said Plain Alice. "Why do you think I spent days and days nursing you back to health?"

"Because I saved your life?" said the boy.

"Oh, do stop throwing that in my face." She softened a little. "Well, that, too."

The boy smiled.

"Forget about your stupid oath," said Plain Alice. "No one else knows but Papa, and he won't say anything."

It was tempting, of course, but the boy knew he could not go back on his word. "I only just discovered that I have honor. If I throw it aside the moment it becomes inconvenient"—he might as well return to High Albemarle and live out his days as a slave—"well, I'm not going to."

"What do you mean, you only just discovered you have honor?" said Plain Alice.

"I meant, uh . . . I meant . . ." It was a perfectly reasonable question. "I meant that you two should wait for me in Middlebury."

"Don't be ridiculous," said Plain Alice. "We're coming with you."

"There's no reason to risk your lives, too," said the boy.

"I am not risking my life. I have every intention of staying out of it," said Mennofar. "I am coming because I have never seen someone burned alive before. One should always be open to new experiences."

"And I'm coming to make sure you don't hurt Ludwig," said Plain Alice.

"Don't hurt Ludwig?" said the boy indignantly.

"Ludwig doesn't want to do all these terrible things. Someone is forcing him," she said. Then she launched into a long explanation of how Ludwig was under the spell of an evil sorcerer. And how he kidnapped her by mistake because he saw names. And how the evil sorcerer who cast the spell bore Ludwig's mark. And how this was all part of a nefarious plot by the evil sorcerer, though the last bit was a little vague as she had no idea what the plot was. "So none of this is Ludwig's fault, which is why you have to promise not to hurt him."

The boy looked down at his lame arm. "I can only use one arm, and the only weapon I have left is a slingshot. How can I hurt him?" he said.

Plain Alice set her jaw. "If you do not take a vow—on your honor—that you won't hurt Ludwig," she said, "I will never, ever speak to you again."

Just the prospect of never speaking to her again made his insides feel hollow. "But he won't have taken the same vow, will he?" asked the boy.

"No," admitted Plain Alice. She thought about it for a moment. "You're just going to have to be the better man, er, creature. Whatever. Now, promise me."

"But—"

"Promise!"

"By the Foul One, you can be a bully when you put your mind to it," said the boy.

"I am protecting the innocent," said Plain Alice. "Besides, you don't know where to find him. I do. Now, take the vow."

The boy had to give in. "On my honor, I vow I'll not hurt Ludwig."

"Too right you won't," said Plain Alice. "I mean, thank you. You made the right choice." She turned around and led them the other way down the Stanhope Road.

10

Plain Alice, Mennofar and the boy walked in silence for a bit. The boy took the chance to go through The Tales to see how he might best a dragon. Usually it took armor, a horse and lance to defeat a dragon, but the boy did not have any of those. Or know how to use them. Something like a magic sword might do. The Tales always made it seem like the countryside was littered with them. Certainly, a proper hero would have gotten hold of one by now, but somehow the boy had failed to find one. And then, there was his promise.

Quite suddenly, Plain Alice blurted out, "If it's just

that you have a really terrible name, like Toad or Wyrm or something, you can tell me." She hurried a bit to close the gap that had opened between the two of them. "I'd keep it a secret. I'm good at keeping secrets."

The boy said, "That's not—"

"I mean, nobody likes their name," said Plain Alice. "Not really."

"I think Alice is a nice name," said the boy.

"Yes, I suppose it is *nice.*" She stuck out her tongue. "Still, it's my ekename I really hate."

"*Plain* Alice," said the boy. "I wondered about that. You're not plain at all." Her pale skin and red hair were striking, particularly to the eyes of an Albemarlman.

Now Plain Alice blushed. "That's not how it's meant," she said. "It's 'plain' as in common, not the Princess," she said.

"Well then, they should call you Just Alice," said the boy. "That'd be better."

"Why?" asked Plain Alice.

The boy said, " 'Just' also means, well"—he did not know how to put the meaning into words—"you know, justice and such."

"Just Alice," she said. "Just Alice. That's pretty good." It would be nice to have an ekename that also meant 'fair' instead of 'not particularly good-looking.' "Just Alice," she said. "Yes, I think I like that. Only when we get back to Middlebury, you have to make sure that everyone hears you call me Just Alice."

"Umm . . . all right," said the boy.

"So it sticks. Everyone will copy you," said Just Alice, answering the question the boy had not asked.

"Why would they copy me?" said the boy.

"Because you'll be a big hero," said Just Alice. "Isn't that why you came and rescued me?"

"No, I did it because of my fate," said the boy.

"Oh, don't tell me you're one of those people who's always on about fate," said Just Alice.

The boy stopped and looked at her. "I don't understand," he said. "Do you mean—are you saying you don't believe in fate?" The boy knew there were people in the world who did not believe in fate, but he had never met one before.

"Why should I?" said Just Alice.

"Because having a fate, even a bad one, is a gift from the gods," said the boy.

"Look, either I have a fate or I don't," said Just Alice. "If I have a fate, then that's what's going to happen to me, whether I believe it's my fate or not—"

"Yes, but—"

"In fact, it'd be my fate not to believe in fate, wouldn't it?"

"No, but—"

"And if I don't have a fate, then I'd be wrong to believe that I did," said Just Alice. "So why should I believe in fate? Either it makes no difference—and I have no choice in the matter—or I'm wrong."

"But—but—but—" spluttered the boy. This was blasphemous in so many different ways he didn't know where to start. "But those who defy their fate are cast into the Pit!"

"Which, by your lights, would be my fate," said Just Alice. "As I don't have any choice in the matter."

Mennofar chuckled. "Got you there, hasn't she?"

"It doesn't work like that," said the boy. It could not.

"Why not?" said Just Alice.

Somehow, Just Alice had managed to take a very simple and beautiful truth and make it twisty and complicated. There was a reason she was wrong. There had to be. "I don't know," said the boy. "But it doesn't."

"Maybe you were fated not to know," said Just Alice.

Mennofar laughed out loud.

"Stop it!" shouted the boy. "I may not be able to explain it, but I know the truth. It's wrong for you to make fun of it."

She put her hand on his shoulder. Very quietly, she said, "I'm sorry."

"It's all right," said the boy. It was not. It was blasphemy. But the boy knew that Alice meant well. And he wanted it to be all right.

"I know I can go on and on, and that gets on people's nerves sometimes," said Just Alice. "Still, it'll do me good if I ever become a sage."

"You can't be a sage," said the boy.

She stiffened. "Because it's not my fate?"

"Because you're a girl," said the boy.

"Girls can be sages!" said Just Alice. "At least, there's no rule against it. It's even happened a few times. I've studied up on it."

"So you're an apprentice sage," said the boy.

"Er, no," said Just Alice, and she explained about agons and ordinaries and extraordinaries. "But they won't invite me. It's like they're just pretending girls are allowed."

"You have to be pretty clever to be a sage," said the boy. Even as he started to say it, he knew he should not. Still, he could not seem to stop himself. "Maybe you're not—"

"They invite every blockhead boy who even thinks about applying!" shouted Just Alice. "I'm smarter than every single one of them!"

"I meant to say maybe they don't realize—"

"I can prove I'm smart enough," she said. "Just give me a problem to solve, if you don't think so."

"I'm sure you're—"

"Give me one!"

"Fine. How do I keep both of my promises?" said the boy. If she was going to start solving problems, they might as well be his problems. "How do I defeat the dragon without hurting him?"

"You're framing the problem wrong," said Just Alice. "You promised to rescue the Princess, not defeat the dragon. You just have to trick the dragon and help the Princess escape. That way, you can keep both promises."

"Oh," said the boy. It was a pretty neat answer, really. And an annoyingly obvious one, once she said it out loud.

"That was easy," said Just Alice. "Now, have you got a hard one?"

"I might," said the boy. There was, of course, no "might" about it. But to explain the problem to her, he would have to tell her about being wrongly enslaved. Still, she might be able to help. In The Tales, there were always parts where the hero stabbed things and parts where the hero figured things out. While he had managed to muddle through his first stabbing part, he had gotten nowhere on figuring things out. "But before I tell you, you have to swear—on *your* honor—not to tell anyone." If she would not, it would be a reason not to tell her.

"I promise," she said.

"And you have to promise not to look down on me or make fun of me or be mean to me," he said.

"That's just ridiculous. Why would someone do that?" she said.

Mennofar did his best to look innocent. The boy just waited.

"All right. I promise," she said.

"I was falsely held as a slave and ran away," said the boy.

"That's terrible," she said. "Who would do such a thing to you?"

"Oh, I have no idea," said the boy.

"Well, how did it happen, then?" asked Just Alice.

"I don't know that, either," said the boy.

"Well, if you don't know—"

"There's a story," said the boy. Then he told her about Casimir's villa and Tibor's murder and Mennofar's rescue and everything else that had happened to him, finishing up with all the yes-or-no questions and the endless scenarios. "Every answer gives me ten more questions. That's the problem," said the boy.

"No, the problem is that you're thick as treacle," snapped Just Alice, smacking him on the head for his stupidity.

The boy said, "But you promised—"

"You've gone about it completely backward. You should be asking the most general questions you can," said Just Alice.

"How would that help?" snapped the boy. He was still stinging from the treacle comment.

"I'll show you. Pick a number between one and thirty," said Just Alice.

"Nineteen," said the boy.

Just Alice rolled her eyes and said, "Pick another one and don't tell me this time." She paused a moment to let him choose. "Now, how many yes-or-no questions do I need to figure out what your number is?"

"Thirty," said the boy. "No, wait, you don't have to ask for the last number, so it's twenty-nine."

Just Alice said, "No, I need—"

"Twenty-eight," said the boy. "You already know it's not nineteen."

Just Alice said, "No, I need—"

"Wait, you said between one and thirty," said the boy. "If that means I can't pick one or thirty, then you need twenty-six."

"Five!" yelled Just Alice. "I need five questions."

The boy said, "Maybe if you were lucky . . ."

"Is your number more than fifteen?" asked Just Alice.

"No," said the boy.

"More than eight?" asked Just Alice.

"Yes," said the boy.

"More than twelve?"

"No."

"More than ten?"

"Yes."

"Is it eleven?"

"No."

"Then it's twelve," said Just Alice. "You just cut the possibilities in half each time."

"That's a good trick," said the boy. "But there's a lot more than thirty possibilities."

"It doesn't matter. More possibilities means you need more questions, but the number of questions does not go up near so fast as the number of possibilities," said Just Alice. "Every time you double the number of possibilities, you need just one more question. Up to thirty-two is five questions, while up to sixty-four is six," she said. "It's all to do with the powers of two."

"I didn't know about the powers of two," said the boy. "I thought it was three and seven that were especially magic. What powers does two have?"

"No, not magical powers," she said. "Powers of two as in doubling each time. It's mathematics— Stop that!"

"Stop what?" said the boy.

"You're nodding along the way people do when they don't want to admit they have no idea what you're talking about," said Just Alice.

The boy stopped nodding.

"But you know what mathematics is, right?" said Just Alice.

The boy said, "Well—"

"Didn't they teach you anything at all?" she said.

"No," said the boy. "Why would they?"

"Why indeed?" she asked. "He wouldn't want a slave who could think, would he?"

"I can think," protested the boy. "I'm not soft."

"No, I didn't mean that," she said. "I just meant that it wouldn't do for him to give you anything to think about."

"Like what?" said the boy.

"Like why some people are slaves and others aren't," said Just Alice.

"Because slave is the fatestone that the Three Sisters drew when those people were born," he said, though she had already made her views on fate clear enough.

"That's not what I meant," said Just Alice.

"Well, what did you mean?" said the boy. "And how did you know which numbers to pick?"

"What? Oh, you just take half the difference between the two numbers. Halfway between ten and twenty is fifteen," said Just Alice.

"And do you memorize those? Because that must take up a lot of your time," said the boy.

"Memorize? No, you just add it up in your head," said Just Alice.

"You can add like that in your head?" asked the boy, wide-eyed.

"Yes. Do you have to write it out?" she asked.

The boy burst out laughing. "I don't know how to write," he said.

"Well then, what do you do?" she said.

"These days, I rescue clever girls from ogres. Before that, I caught bats for goblins. And before that, I took care of the plants in the inner and outer courtyards," said the boy.

"Yes. Of course. Stupid question, really," she said, mostly to herself. "Anyway, the point is to start broad and eliminate lots of possibilities at a single stroke."

"I know," said the boy. "I can remember that much."

"From when? Before you were born?" said Just Alice.

"Don't be such a mean-o," said the boy. "I remember it from when you showed me a minute ago." He scowled at her. "You think I'm just some ignorant slaveboy, don't you? Maybe I never did study with *sages,* but that doesn't mean I can't learn something when shown it. I'm not stupid."

"I don't think that," said Just Alice, sounding as though she might. "Now, if you're not a slave, then either you were born free or you were born a slave and then freed. So find out which."

"I must have been born free," said the boy. He had an important fate, and there was no way it could be if he were just some freed slave.

"Just ask," said Just Alice.

"Fine," said the boy. He turned to Mennofar. "I was born free, wasn't I?"

Neither of them had noticed that Mennofar was aiming a fearsome scowl at Just Alice or that his skin had turned a green so dark it was almost black. "No," he said.

"You got it wrong," said the boy. "The answer was supposed to be yes."

"No, it wasn't," said Mennofar.

"It has to be," said the boy. "I can't be a freed slave. I have an important fate. You told me so. Somebody stole it from me and tried to destroy the proof." He waved the ring. "The only way I have a birthright worth stealing is if I was born free."

Mennofar shrugged.

"Don't shrug at me," said the boy. "You're saying I'm a freed slave?"

"No, no, no, no," cried out Just Alice in frustration. "The point is not to waste questions like that. You already know that you are free and that you were not born free. That has—"

"No," said Mennofar.

"—to mean you were freed after you were born. Asking if you were is totally unnecessary and— Wait, did he say no?" said Just Alice.

"I did," said Mennofar. He gave her his toothiest smile. His skin shot from near black to a shade of emerald that almost glowed.

"You said it was about eliminating lots of possibilities," said the boy. "What happens when you eliminate all of them?"

"I don't know," said Just Alice.

Just Alice and the boy both studied Mennofar for a long moment. Mennofar just glowed back at them with his happy green glow.

"He told me once that humans and goblins are too different to ever really be friends," said the boy.

"Mennofar, you're a good goblin. Won't you give us a hint?" said Just Alice.

"Doing anything more than holding to my exact word would be a stain upon my honor as a goblin," said

Mennofar. "Besides, your little logic lesson put a big dent in my fun. Why should I give up any more of it?"

"Rot," said the boy. "We don't even know what to ask. You're having more fun than when I was asking the wrong questions."

"That *could* be true," admitted Mennofar.

That evening, they camped only a little ways short of where Ludwig once held Just Alice prisoner. They ate a cold meal and turned in early. Just Alice, however, couldn't sleep. She lay on her back and looked up at the sea of stars overhead. In the morning, they would rise, and the boy would face a dragon, a dragon he had taken a mighty oath not to harm. A few hours before, that oath had been so important to her, but now it just seemed ridiculous to tie his hands like that. Of course, there probably wasn't any way he *could* hurt Ludwig, but she still shouldn't have demanded it of him. "I'm sorry," she said in a voice barely above a whisper.

"For what?" came the boy's voice back through the darkness.

"For—I don't know," said Just Alice. "For being so bossy. I can't help it. It just comes over me sometimes."

"I don't think you're bossy," said the boy.

"It's sweet of you to say so," said Just Alice. "But I know the truth."

"I really don't," said the boy.

Just Alice laughed a little.

"What's so funny?" said the boy.

"It just struck me: how would you even know if I was bossy?" said Just Alice. "You were a slave."

The boy shot up. "That's not true!" he said.

"No, I meant—"

"Take it back!" said the boy. "It's a lie."

Mennofar sighed heavily. "I suspect she meant that because you were generally believed to be a slave, you were likely accustomed to being ordered around," he said. "So it is unlikely that you would be the best judge of whether someone was, or was not, bossy."

"Oh," said the boy, mollified. "That does make sense, I guess." He lay back down. For a long moment, no one said anything. "I never thought about it that way before," he said finally. His voice was very quiet. "I guess they did like to give me orders. They sure did it a lot."

Just Alice reached out and took his hand in the dark. "I know," she said.

"Yes, yes, I am sure it was terrible. Now, will you please go to sleep," said Mennofar. "You have a big day ahead of you, and you will not want to be tired and cranky when the dragon roasts you alive."

In the morning, ten minutes' walk brought the boy, Just Alice and Mennofar to the strange patch of broken ground where basalt columns reached up toward the sky—the place where Just Alice had been imprisoned only a few days earlier. Sure enough, on top of the tallest column, a pretty young girl was marooned in the wreck of an expensive silk dress. It had been torn by dragon claws, stained with sheep's blood and generally ruined by a week's camping in the wild. The three of them crept forward and hid behind a boulder.

Just Alice peeked over the top. "I don't see Ludwig," she whispered.

"Is it the Princess?" asked the boy.

"Who else would it be?" asked Just Alice.

From atop the pillar of stone came a lordly pronouncement. "Oh, I grow ever so weary of mutton."

"She sounds like a princess," said Mennofar. "And I have known a few."

"And did you torture them as bad as you're torturing me?" asked the boy.

Mennofar thought for a moment. "Some, yes," he said.

Just Alice peered around the rock. "I don't see him. I don't think he's even here," she said.

"Then who was she talking to?" said the boy.

"I don't know," whispered Just Alice. "Maybe she's expecting someone to bring her lunch." She stood up and surveyed the scene.

From behind one of the boulders, Ludwig's head bobbed up. Slowly, the great spade-tipped tail uncoiled. His bat wings unfurled, and when the boulder itself began to rise and turn, she could see it was actually

Ludwig's broad hindquarters. He turned himself all the way around and faced Just Alice head-on. Through all the time she spent with Ludwig, she had never stood on level ground with him. She had never taken in just how big he was. He was bigger than a house, and his claws were the size of full-grown men. Each of his wickedly sharp teeth was the length of her arm.

"Oh, dear, it's you, isn't it?" said Ludwig. "I'm sorry. I was rather fond of you." Just Alice did not like the way he spoke in the past tense.

11

Just Alice drew herself up to her full height, set her jaw firmly and cast a cool eye on Ludwig. "Yes, I am Just Alice," she said.

"I thought you were Plain Alice," said Ludwig, a little confused. "Who changed it?"

"No one," said Just Alice. "Er, I mean, I did."

Ludwig studied her quizzically. "But it *is* you, right?" he said. "You are the same Alice I carried off before, aren't you?"

"Yes," she said. "I escaped from the ogre."

Ludwig set his head on the ground and put his two

front paws on his snout. "That is good," he said. "But why did you come here? Couldn't you just have gone home?"

"Not while you still hold the Princess," said Just Alice.

"Who?" said Ludwig.

"The Princess. Up on the stone pillar. The other Alice," said Just Alice.

"Oh, her, right. Sorry," said Ludwig. He glanced back and forth between Just Alice and the Princess. "It's confusing."

Peeking out from behind the rock, the boy saw that Ludwig was confused. But apart from being about the same age, the two Alices did not look much alike. "He really can't tell them apart," whispered the boy to Mennofar. Ludwig's ears twitched ever so slightly as the boy whispered.

"We have come to rescue the Princess," said Just Alice. Bold words did not keep her voice from trembling a little.

"We?" said Ludwig. "Who else is with you?"

Behind the rock, Mennofar and the boy froze. "No one," said Just Alice. "It's just a manner of speaking."

"But who were you talking to earlier, then?" said Ludwig.

"No one," she said. "I told you."

Ludwig wrinkled his brow and turned to the rock. He studied it for a long moment and said, "Come out from behind that rock, Mennofarlaksojardigonairejigroarfavis-cogumegomoffkilgerspio—"

"Mennofar is fine," said Mennofar. He popped out from behind the rock. "It will take several hours to say the whole thing."

The boy braced himself to be called out by Ludwig as well, but Ludwig said, "Very well, Mennofar. You are a brave goblin to come here."

"How dare you!" said Mennofar. "I can assure you I am a complete coward."

"Then you did not come to rescue Alice?"

"No," said Mennofar, "I thought it was a terrible idea."

"I," said Just Alice, pausing for a moment, "and I alone, have come to stop you."

Ludwig raised his head. "Have you really? How?"

"Well, I'm not actually sure," said Just Alice.

"Oh," said Ludwig. He sagged back down. "I was hoping you had figured something out."

"Foul beast, your nefarious schemes will come to naught," cried the Princess.

"She talks like that a lot," said Ludwig to Just Alice. He turned to the Princess. "I keep explaining to you that the nefarious schemes are not mine. They belong to the one who has summoned me. I am bound to his will by an enchantment which no one can free me from."

"Vile worm, I will be saved by a brave prince," said

Princess Alice. Out of the corner of her eye, she studied the boy. "Or perhaps a knight"—she paused—"or squire? . . . Page?"

"What are you looking at?" said Ludwig. He turned to stare at the boulder again. "Those old rags?"

And with that, the boy knew he had something better than a spell or a magic weapon. He had no name. Ludwig could not see him. It was as good as having a ring of invisibility, and in The Tales, rings of invisibility were used for all manner of tricks. The boy started to stand up.

"What are you doing?" whispered Mennofar.

"I don't have a name," whispered the boy. "So he can't see me."

"Yes, but he will see your trousers dancing around in front of him, and what will he think of that?" whispered Mennofar.

The boy stopped. He had not thought of that. "What should I do?"

"Take them off, thickwit," whispered Mennofar.

"You mean—" The boy blushed violently. "Not in front of the girls."

Mennofar sighed.

"Who are you whispering to?" demanded Ludwig.

"No one," said Mennofar. "I mean, myself. I mutter to myself sometimes."

Ludwig eyed Mennofar. "That sounded more like whispering than muttering," he said.

"Well, it can be a subtle distinction," said Mennofar.

"Mennofar, I can't," whispered the boy. "Not with them watching."

In a booming voice, Mennofar said, "Ladies, would you please cover your eyes until I direct you to do otherwise."

"Is this some kind of trick?" asked Ludwig.

"It is indeed a trick, and a very entertaining one, but it is a trick I will need the ladies to close their eyes for," said Mennofar.

Both girls put their hands over their eyes. Mennofar nodded to the boy. First the boy took his father's ring from around his neck, giving it a quick rub as he did so. Then, very gingerly, the boy slipped his arm out of the sling. Finally, he skinned out of his trousers. He could only use his good arm, so it was a good thing that the trousers were so large. He took a deep breath to fortify his nerve and stepped out from behind the boulder. As soon as they caught a glimpse of him, both girls squealed and squeezed shut the gaps they had deliberately left between their fingers.

For a long moment, the boy simply stood in front of Ludwig. Mennofar glanced back and forth between the boy and Ludwig. But Ludwig did not pounce on the boy. He just sat there. The boy took a few steps.

"Well," said Ludwig. "What's thc trick?"

The boy walked right past Ludwig. Or he would've, if he hadn't tripped over a rock and fallen flat on his face.

"Who's there?" said Ludwig.

"No one," said the boy. He slammed his hands over his mouth, but it was too late.

"Idiot," muttered Just Alice.

Mennofar palmed his face.

But Ludwig wrinkled his brow. "Is this the trick?" he said.

"Yes," said the boy. He stood up. Projecting his voice as forcefully as he could, he said, "I am no one."

Ludwig homed in on the boy's voice. "How can you be no one?" he said.

"Who is right in front of you?" said the boy.

"No one," said Ludwig. "But that does not make any sense." He wrinkled his formidable brow. "When one says 'no one,' one means the absence of any entity. How can there be a 'no one'?"

"I can prove that I am no one," said the boy. "You can see the names of all things. If I am not no one, if I am someone, you can see my name. Therefore, I challenge you, O dragon, to say my name," said the boy.

Ludwig sat for a moment and studied the spot where the boy stood. As the boy looked back at Ludwig, he had a queasy thought. He might actually have a name. His parents, whoever they were, could have given him one when he was too little to remember or even after he was taken from them. Ludwig had not seen his name yet, but that might not mean anything. For all the boy knew, names rarely used might be very small and hard to see. Ludwig might find it as soon as he looked hard enough.

The boy held his breath. Ludwig's head floated right in front of him. The tiniest lick of flame would be the end of him.

Finally, Ludwig said, "I cannot." He bowed his head a little. "I do not understand how, but you are no one."

The boy exhaled in relief.

At the same time, he was a little disturbed. His parents should have named him, even if they thought he was dead. Their failure to do so suggested a certain cavalier attitude toward their duties as parents. He had to wonder if he really wanted to find parents like that.

Still, he had to deal with Ludwig, so he set aside those thoughts for later. Drawing in his breath, he said, "Ludwig, I free you from your bonds."

Ludwig said, "Free me? But—"

"Once a dragon is bound, no one may free it," said the boy. He took a deep breath. If this didn't work, there was going to be a lot of trouble. "I am no one, and I free you. Go! You are free!"

Ludwig took a dainty step away from the Princess. When nothing happened, he took a bigger step. And another. Then he bounded off a fair distance. Still nothing happened. Ludwig glanced about and leapt into the sky. All four of them were scoured by the torrents of dust kicked up by the beating of his wings. He flew a mile or more away, wheeled about and flew back over them. "No one has freed me," he called down to them. "Thank you, Alice. Thank you, Mennofar. Thank you for bringing me no one." Slowly, Ludwig's mighty wings carried him higher and higher into the sky and farther and farther to the north.

"That's it?" said the Princess.

"That was brilliant, absolutely brilliant," said Just Alice.

"Well done, lad. Worthy of a goblin," said Mennofar, and offered the boy his hand.

The boy shook Mennofar's hand. "You know, I wasn't sure that was going to work," he said. Then he saw that both Alices were staring at him. He yelped, covered himself with his hands and darted behind the rock to get dressed again.

Just Alice went to the pillar. "We have to get her down and get out of here before Ludwig comes back," she said.

Dressed again, the boy came out from behind the boulder. "Back?" he said. "Why would he come back?"

"Because of the spell," said Just Alice. "I assume it'll only let him go so far."

"But the spell is broken," said the boy. "I freed him."

"You were very clever," said Just Alice, "but all you did was use a load of nonsense to trick him."

"How was that nonsense?" said the boy. It really was not fair. She wanted him to use logic, and when he did, she told him it was a lot of nonsense. There was no winning with her.

"No one has no name. You have no name. Therefore, you are no one. That's wrong," said Just Alice. "It's like saying the Princess's name is Alice, and my name is Alice. Therefore, I am the Princess. It's what's called a fallacy."

"But, but—"

"Which you should know because you are *not* no one," said Just Alice. "And don't get me started on reification—"

"Maybe the spell was supposed to be broken by a person without a name," said the boy. "Magic's always a bit peculiar."

"Perhaps there was no spell," said Mennofar. "Maybe he was bound solely by his own belief." He gave the boy a meaningful look.

"He'd have to be pretty dumb to fall for that," said the boy. "Poof. You have to do whatever I say. Why? Because I say so."

"It's not hard to see right through that," said Just Alice.

The Princess called out, "Gallant peons, were we not just discoursing on the subject of . . ." She trailed off as if she did not know what to say next. "Oh, just get me down!" And she burst into tears.

Just Alice showed the Princess how to get down. Although the Princess was reluctant to try, she managed quite gracefully. More gracefully than Just Alice had, which Just Alice found strangely irritating.

When she was safely on the ground, the Princess took a moment and composed herself. Then, addressing the boy, Just Alice and Mennofar, she said, "Stout yeoman, stalwart maid, loyal, uh . . . goblin, you have delivered me from the clutches of a noxious creature, an act of valor and fortitude for which you have my eternal thanks. Let us away unto fair Farnham, where my father the King will reward you all richly and handsomely. Now, conduct me unto my carriage."

"Carriage?" said the boy.

"Yes, so that I may be conveyed back to Farnham in a manner befitting my station in life."

There was a long, silent moment.

The Princess looked around the blasted and desolate country. "Then perhaps a palanquin?" she suggested without much real hope.

"What's that?" asked Just Alice.

"It's a sort of box you get in and slaves carry you around," said the boy.

"No palanquins," said Just Alice. "We're on foot."

"Very well," said the Princess. "I shall not complain about these tribulations, as the great majority of my future subjects travel our lands on their feet. For a monarch, or a future monarch, to learn of the ways of the people is the source of great wisdom, and—"

"The way you go on," said Just Alice. No sooner had she said it than she realized she had spoken out of turn. "Er, I mean, the way Your Highness does go on." That was not much better.

But the Princess dropped the lofty tones, fancy accent and arch diction. "You don't like the way I talk?" she said.

"I'm sorry, Your Highness, it's just that when you go on and on like that, you sound a little pompous," said Just Alice. "Doesn't she?" said Just Alice to the boy.

The boy looked away, while Mennofar just hummed a little tune.

"Er, I'm sure you're a very nice person," said Just Alice.

"Well, how am I to know what to do?" said the Princess. "Father is always after me to be less frivolous and act like a queen, and the Chamberlain says that's how people want royalty to talk, and you say I sound ridiculous and pompous, and, and"—she burst out crying all over again—"and I'm cold and tired and hungry, and I was kidnapped by a dragon who wouldn't shut up about how clever that other Alice was." Her tears streaked the dirt on her face.

"Would you like us to take you home?" the boy asked gently.

"Yes!" bawled the Princess.

"Then let's go," he said. He took her hand in his and led her away, leaving Just Alice and Mennofar to scurry after them.

When the Princess stopped crying, she wiped her face with the sleeves of her dress. Whether this made her face any cleaner was debatable. "I was wondering something," she said to the boy. "You said palanquins are carried by slaves, but what are slaves?"

"You don't know what slaves are?" said the boy.

"How can you be so ig— How can you not know that?" said Just Alice.

"Is it unpleasant?" said the Princess. "The Chamberlain ordered my tutors not to teach me about anything unpleasant. He says that it is unbecoming for young ladies to know about unpleasant things."

"Slaves are people who are owned by someone else, their master," said Mennofar. "The master gets to decide everything, and the slaves just have to do what they are ordered to."

"That doesn't sound very nice," said Princess Alice. "I hope it pays well, at least."

"It doesn't pay at all," said Just Alice. "It's not a job."

"That's terrible," said the Princess. "I would never agree to be a slave."

"It isn't something you get to decide," said the boy. "You're just born that way."

"If I were a slave," said the Princess, "I wouldn't follow any of their stupid orders."

"Then they'd whip you," said the boy.

"I'd run away," said the Princess.

"Then they'd hang you," said the boy.

"That's awful," said the Princess. She shuddered. "It all sounds awful. When we get home, you must tell

Father so he can do something about it. He is the King, you know."

"It is just possible that he already knows," said Mennofar.

"No, he would have done something about it," said the Princess. "The Chamberlain must be keeping it secret from him, too." She thought about this a moment more. "I'm beginning to wonder if the Chamberlain might not be entirely trustworthy."

"Never mind all that," said the boy. Talking about slavery made him nervous. "We need to keep a lookout for the next monster."

"What next monster?" said Just Alice.

"In The Tales, there are always three monsters to be defeated, each more fearsome than the last," said the boy. "So ogre, dragon, and then what?"

"The Tales are a load of old nonsense parents use to get little children to eat spinach," said Just Alice. "Now, let's get to Castle Geoffrey, where it's safe."

12

Duke Geoffrey sat atop his great black warhorse and surveyed his courtyard full of men. They were almost ready to depart, but they had *been* almost ready for over an hour. Still, they kept adjusting their saddles or fiddling with their luggage straps or dawdling over nonexistent tasks. It was tempting to ride off and leave them all behind, but he could not. Duke Geoffrey had every intention of appearing to heroically best the dragon in single combat and rescue Princess Alice. And appearances need witnesses. So he sat and waited.

"Your Grace, Your Grace," puffed the Majordomo. He hurried to Duke Geoffrey's side, red-faced and gasping. "Your Grace, the Princess is here."

"Princess Alice?" said Duke Geoffrey. He slid from his saddle. "Then the dragon is defeated?"

"By your glorious martial prowess, no doubt," said the nearest man-at-arms. "Three cheers for the Duke. Hip—"

Duke Geoffrey clouted the man on the back of the head. "Silence, dolt." He turned back to the Majordomo and said, "Take me to her."

The Majordomo led Duke Geoffrey to the gate. "May it please Your Grace," he said, "I present Her Royal Highness the Princess Alice, and her retinue"—he glanced at her three companions—"a local girl, a ragamuffin and"—he took a second look—"their pet tree frog, perhaps?"

The Princess was dirty. Her clothes were tattered and stained. And she was keeping company with the Earl's absurd champion and his pet. But it was her. That much was beyond doubt. Duke Geoffrey swallowed hard. Something had gone gravely awry. Somehow, that simpering twit of a dragon had actually managed to let the Earl's preposterous gutter urchin defeat him, wrecking Duke Geoffrey's carefully laid plans in the process. Still, there was an opportunity in this defeat. His father always said that fortune favors the bold, but Duke Geoffrey had found that she also looks kindly on the flexible. And without knowing it, his enemy had just delivered herself into his hands.

Duke Geoffrey put on his best face and swept Princess Alice up in his arms. "Sweet cousin, to know that you are back safe in our protection brings such gladness to my heart."

"Dear cousin," said Princess Alice, "it weighs heavily upon us to think that our petty cares burdened you with any worries."

"So kind, so selfless," said Duke Geoffrey. He took hold of her shoulder and steered her toward the main hall. Her companions and the Majordomo all fell in behind them. "Now, if you will forgive some meddling by an older relative, I should like to speak of the future. You are, after all, of age."

"Not quite," said Princess Alice.

"Close enough, though, that you must have given some consideration to the question of your matrimonial prospects," said Duke Geoffrey.

"Happy we are to address these matters," said the Princess. "There are gladsome tidings, for I am newly engaged to be wed."

"What! Who?" said Duke Geoffrey. It was not possible. There might have been some discussions with Crown Prince Edgar of East Stanhope, but the King could not have actually made an agreement without Duke Geoffrey's spies at court getting wind of it.

"Why, my rescuer and champion, of course," she said, and pointed to the boy.

"Me?" said the boy.

"Him!" shouted Duke Geoffrey in surprise.

"He has rescued me from a terrible monster and has declared his intention to ask for my hand in marriage as his boon," said the Princess.

"You?" said Duke Geoffrey to the boy. The idea was ridiculous. She was a princess of the realm, and he was—quite literally—no one.

"Yes, Your Grace," said the boy. His voice cracked a little.

"Your father will never consent," said Duke Geoffrey to the Princess.

"He must," said the Princess. "To refuse my rescuer his reward would be a scandal." She was a proper lady, so she patted her forehead with her handkerchief at the mere mention of scandal.

No matter how preposterous the suggestion was, she was right. It would be difficult for King Julian to refuse. "But he has nothing to his name," said the Duke. "He doesn't even *have* a name."

"I am quite certain that my father can grant him a name to go with lands and titles," said the Princess.

Duke Geoffrey took in a long breath. Nothing could be gained from arguing about this. "Yes, of course," said the Duke through gritted teeth. "Refusal would be totally out of the question." He studied the boy for a moment.

The last time they'd met, he had taken the boy for a joke. That was his mistake. Now he saw what the boy really was: an obstacle to be eliminated. Duke Geoffrey smiled as broadly as he could force himself to. "But this is a joyous occasion," he said. "We must celebrate with a feast in honor of the doubly happy news of rescue and wedding."

"A feast?" said the boy, a little uncertainly.

"You will be my guests of honor," said Duke Geoffrey. "You cannot refuse."

"No," said Princess Alice. "I don't believe we can."

"Excellent," said Duke Geoffrey. He snapped his fingers at the Majordomo. "You will take care of matters."

"Yes, Your Grace," said the Majordomo.

"And after you have shown our guests to their quarters, return to me," said Duke Geoffrey. "There are a few *special* arrangements to be discussed."

"Yes, Your Grace." The Majordomo bowed and smiled to show that he took Duke Geoffrey's meaning. He was the perfect man to carry out the Duke's latest scheme.

The Majordomo led the Princess, Just Alice, Mennofar and the boy into the keep and down a corridor. "Your Highness, I know you will all be a little dusty from the road. So we will draw hot baths for each of you," said the Majordomo. "And I see that you and your, er, lady-in-waiting will need fresh dresses. We haven't many ladies here in the castle, but I'm sure we will be able to find something for you to borrow. I must ask your forgiveness if it is not up to the latest fashions, Your Highness." He smiled unctuously.

The Princess smiled back. "Think nothing of it. I most certainly understand," she said. After a pause, she added, "Given how far we are from the royal court."

The Majordomo clenched his teeth. "Just as you say, Your Highness."

The boy walked a few steps behind them and wondered if he was really supposed to marry the Princess. A hero from The Tales would jump at the chance to marry a princess, *if* he wasn't a prince himself. Of course, the boy didn't know what he was, so he wasn't sure what he was supposed to do. Still, he knew better than to contradict the Princess. A story, once told, must be stuck to no matter what. That rule the boy had learned early on in Casimir's house, even if it was not one of the Ninety-Nine Duties.

The Majordomo stopped at a set of doors and called back, "Ladies, your baths await." The Princess and Just Alice were admitted by a chambermaid. The Majordomo led Mennofar and the boy to a second set of doors. "You two can freshen up in here," he said.

Before he could leave, the boy stopped him. "Sir, I was wondering if you could help me, too."

The Majordomo tilted his head back so he could look all the way down his nose at the boy. "With what?"

"This is all I have to wear," said the boy. "And it's not really the proper sort of thing for a feast. Do you think I could borrow something, too? Even just a shirt?"

"Oh, I see, yes," said the Majordomo. "Well, don't you worry about that." He patted the boy awkwardly on the head. Then he made a show of dusting his hands off. "I'm sure we'll be able to arrange something appropriate for you." Before anything more could be said, he hustled Mennofar and the boy into the room and slammed the door after them.

In the room was a round wooden tub of water, with fresh towels and a large cake of soap set out beside it. Thin trails of steam rose off of the water.

"A hot bath," said Mennofar. "What could be more civilized?"

"I wouldn't know," said the boy. He had never taken a bath before.

"None of that, now." They turned to see a large iron-haired woman with her sleeves rolled up. She had a wicked scrub brush in one hand. "His Grace wants you clean as a whistle," she said. "Now, skin out of them clothes."

"What?" said the boy.

"Don't make a fuss, now," she said. "I've nine sons and twenty-five grandsons. You've nothing I ain't seen before." The boy barely had time to undress before she hoisted him in the air and tipped him headfirst into the tub. She might have been a grandmother, but she had the strength of a blacksmith. She scrubbed him so hard he thought his skin was going to come off, and shoved him under the water when he protested. She did slow down and proceed gingerly when she came to his bad arm. Otherwise, she scoured him viciously.

Mennofar cackled with laughter. At least, he did until the old woman, finally satisfied with how clean the boy was, released him and grabbed Mennofar. Mennofar cried out, "Madam, I must pro—" Then he was underwater.

The boy wrapped one of the towels around his waist and watched as Mennofar was put through the same torture he had endured. "You'll need another three vows to escape her," he said.

Mennofar choked out, "I fail to see"—dunk—"the humor in"—dunk—"these proceedings!" Dunk.

"Oh, this green do stick, don't it?" said the old woman. "Just what did you get into, you naughty little boy?" When she finally decided that no amount of vigorous scrubbing was going to take the green off the goblin, she gave up and let him go.

Mennofar leapt from the tub, wrapped a towel around himself like a toga and said, "Woman, I am over six hundred years old, and in all of my six centuries, never—*never,* I say—have I been visited upon by such shocking indignities." He raised his tiny fist and waved it at her.

"Oh, you look just like a wee angry man," said the old woman. "Aren't you the cutest little thing?" She bent down and plastered a wet kiss on top of his head.

Mennofar spluttered in rage but could not manage to get out anything coherent.

The old woman turned back to the boy and said, "Let's have a go at that hair, then." She planted the boy on a bench and went to work. It was the first time in his life his hair had ever been brushed. When he had been a slave in Casimir's house, the boy's hair had been kept close to the scalp. But since his escape, it had grown into a wild tangle of curls. Now the boy paid dearly for it. The old woman was not to be denied. She laid into his hair with a brush until it was completely untangled, beat the curls into enough of a semblance of submission that she could part his hair right down the middle and stepped back to survey her work. Wetting her thumb in her mouth, she damped down one remaining errant curl. When it met her approval, she said, "That's just how them fancy lads at court wears it." This had not been true for at least a quarter of a century.

"And what about the young miss?" said the lady's maid.

Just Alice snapped awake. The hot bath had left her feeling warm and drowsy. She must have dozed off while the lady's maid fixed the Princess's hair.

The lady's maid thumped the empty seat in front of a large vanity. The vanity was heavily laden with combs and brushes and scissors and odd devices that had to be used to curl hair. There were all sorts of creams and powders, each in its own little pot. "Would the young miss like me to do up her hair?"

"Yes, of course," she said. She jumped up and took the empty seat in front of the mirror.

The lady's maid studied Just Alice's hair and frowned a little. She rubbed a lock between her fingers to feel how thick it was. "And how does the young miss like to wear it?"

"Well, I brush it every morning," said Just Alice, though this did not seem like a particularly helpful comment.

"But for special occasions?" said the Princess. "For court dances and formal dinners?"

"Um," said Just Alice. She had never been to a court dance or a formal dinner. "Er . . ." She fumbled for the name of even one hairstyle.

"Perhaps the young miss would like some ideas for something new to try?"

"Yes!" Just Alice grabbed onto the suggestion. "Something new for once." She waved her hand to dismiss all the tired old hairstyles she had never actually worn. She disliked not knowing things.

The lady's maid studied her head for another moment. "Perhaps a crown braid?"

The Princess exploded. “A crown braid! Have you lost your mind?”

The lady’s maid started in surprise. “But, Your Highness,” she said, “what is wrong with—”

“Is it not enough that circumstances compel me to attend this feast without my crown?” spat the Princess, advancing on the lady’s maid. “Now you want to call attention to that fact by braiding my companion’s hair into the shape of the very thing I am denied?”

“I’m sorry, Your Highness,” said the lady’s maid, taking a step back. “I didn’t think—”

“Get out!” screamed the Princess. “Now!” Her wrath was terrifying to behold, and the lady’s maid fled the room in tears. When it was clear that the maid was not coming back, the Princess’s anger vanished just as quickly as it had appeared. She gently shut the door and took the lady’s maid’s spot behind Just Alice. “I’ll do your hair while—”

Just Alice turned to face the Princess. “You can’t treat people like that!” she said.

The Princess stared at Just Alice in surprise. “Like what?”

“First you bully the boy into agreeing to marry you, and then you terrorize that poor girl when she was just trying to do her job,” said Just Alice.

“Who?” said the Princess. She glanced back at the door. “Oh, her. She’ll be fine. I just needed to speak to you without any spies lurking around.”

"She's a lady's maid," said Just Alice. "Not a spy." But as soon as she said it aloud, she realized that if the Duke wanted to spy on them, a lady's maid was exactly who he'd send.

"And I was only pretending about the marriage," said the Princess.

"Were you really?" asked Just Alice. The news lightened her heart, which was strange. There was no reason it should matter to her. "Why?"

"We are all in grave danger," said the Princess. "Geoffrey is fighting with my father over whether I will inherit the throne or he will." She turned Just Alice back around to face the mirror and began to plait her hair. "When I saw that Geoffrey was going to ask for my hand, I had to invent an obstacle that even he could not overcome. So I pretended I was already bound to marry my rescuer."

"That's pretty clever, really," said Just Alice.

"I got the idea from Geoffrey's sister," said the Princess. "She was rescued from an ogre by some knight. He demanded her hand in marriage. She didn't like him at all, but she had to do it anyway."

"Poor girl," said Just Alice.

"I'm sure Geoffrey wanted to rescue me himself so he could do the same thing," said the Princess. "I saw it as soon as he asked about my marriage prospects."

"How can you catch all that and still have no idea what a slave is?" said Just Alice.

"How can you know what reification is and still miss all that?" said the Princess.

It was a fair point, but Just Alice was not about to admit it. She crossed her arms and leveled her nastiest glare at the Princess.

The Princess looked at Just Alice forlornly. "I wish I could scowl like that," she said. "People would take me so much more seriously."

Just Alice tried mightily to keep glowering, but the tiniest snort of a laugh escaped her. In response, the Princess giggled a little. It was only a little, but it was enough. They both collapsed in a fit of laughter that left them gasping for breath and wiping the tears from their eyes.

When the Princess regained a little of her composure, she looked at Just Alice's reflection in the mirror. "You know, with the shape of your face, a crown braid really would be just the thing," she said.

Just Alice clapped her hands over her mouth to keep herself from laughing again. "You can't!" she said through a barely contained chortle. "Not after what you put that poor girl through."

The Princess fought back against her own giggles. It was a mighty struggle, but in the end, she won. "You're right, of course," she said with forced calm. She began pinning Just Alice's plaits up into a bun. "We need to be serious. And we need the boy to play along, just till we leave in the morning."

"I'll explain it to him," said Just Alice.

"You have to warn him, too," said the Princess. "Duke Geoffrey is going to do everything he can to make trouble between now and tomorrow morning."

♠

"Get up, boy. Get up. We need to get going," said the Majordomo, shaking him awake.

The boy pulled back the towel that Mennofar had draped over him like a blanket. He sat up and rubbed his eyes. "How long was I asleep?" he asked.

"Oh, a few hours," said Mennofar. His raiment had transformed itself into a black tailcoat, white bow tie and starched white shirt.

"Let's go. Let's go," chivvied the Majordomo.

"I need to get dressed," said the boy. All he had on was the towel wrapped around his middle.

The Majordomo glanced about the room. "Arrangements were made. Arrangements were made. Why has nothing been delivered?" He put his head out the door. "Nurse!"

The old woman came in another door. Under her arm was a package wrapped in paper and tied up in string. "It's here," she said. "Came just now."

"At last," said the Majordomo. He seized the package from her and shoved it into the boy's arms.

"Thank you," said the boy. He unwrapped the package. It contained the same tatty pair of trousers that he had been wearing for months. He looked up at the Majordomo.

"We had them cleaned and pressed," said the Majordomo, evidently quite pleased with his handiwork. "Good as new."

They were not.

"These here are the Duke's guests," said the old woman. "You can't send the lad to a feast wearing that, you toffee-headed fool. It'd be a black mark on the Duke's hospitality."

"Mind your tongue, you old bat," said the Majordomo. "I can have you turned out of this castle in a heartbeat."

"Just you go and try," said the old woman. "You'll find out who the Duke loves more, you or his old nurse." She crossed her arms and glared at the Majordomo.

The Majordomo pursed his lips but said nothing.

"What I thought," said the old woman. "Now, go and borrow the boy something decent to wear."

"As it happens, madam," said the Majordomo, "I personally investigated that possibility. Unfortunately, no one has anything more suitable to lend him."

"In a castle with hundreds of men and boys?" she said.

"Yes," said the Majordomo through clenched teeth.

She stared at him for a long moment, but this time, he met her gaze. "Bring shame on the Duke's name for a generation to come," she muttered as she turned and left.

The Majordomo turned back to the boy and clapped his hands lightly. "Now, let's get dressed. We cannot keep the feast waiting," he said.

The boy looked down at the trousers. All the guests at the feast would be dressed in their finest, and he would have to wear these rags. "The Duke probably wants to visit with his cousin," he said. "Maybe I shouldn't go."

"Not go? Not go!" said the Majordomo. "You are the guest of honor. To refuse to go would be a grievous insult to the Duke."

The boy looked to Mennofar. Mennofar shook his head.

The boy sighed and got dressed.

The Majordomo led the two of them back to the suite where they had left Just Alice and the Princess. He knocked on the door and said, "Ladies?"

The door opened. Steam wafted out, carrying the smell of lavender and fresh soap. Just Alice emerged, followed by the Princess. They were completely transformed. Gone were their torn and filthy dresses. Instead, they wore beautiful silk gowns. And their hair had been done up in complicated arrangements involving combs and pins and ribbons and flowers and such.

The boy gawped at them. "You look beautiful," he said.

"You don't have to act so surprised," said Just Alice, but then she smiled a little.

"Why are you wearing that?" said the Princess. "You are to be my fiancé."

"I'm sorry," said the boy.

"What are you apologizing for?" said the Princess. Rounding on the Majordomo, she said, "This is an insult."

"Madam, I fear you overlook the fact that you are a guest," said the Majordomo. "Do not forget that your place is—"

"At the right hand of my father, His Majesty, the King," said the Princess. "Might it not be that you are the one who has forgotten his place?"

Not all bullies are cowards, but the Majordomo was. "Yes, Your Highness. Very sorry, Your Highness. Great stain on the Duke's honor, just as you said," he groveled. Then he bounded ahead to escape the conversation.

To the boy, the Princess said, "I'm so sorry. This is all my fault."

"Your fault?" said the boy, but the Princess was already headed after the Majordomo.

"The Duke is insulting you," whispered Just Alice.

"Again," whispered Mennofar.

"He could have found something for you if he wanted to," whispered Just Alice. "And that'll only be the beginning. The Duke wants to marry the Princess so he can become king."

"But I'm going to marry the Princess," said the boy. "Or am I? I'm getting confused."

"It's perfectly simple. The Princess only said that she was marrying you to keep the Duke from trying to force her to agree to marry him. But the Duke doesn't know that, of course. So he's going to try to make trouble to keep you from marrying the Princess, even though that isn't really going to happen. So you must not fail to keep the Duke from preventing that from not happening." The words tumbled out of Just Alice in a rush. When she'd gotten it all out, she looked at the boy expectantly.

"Um," said the boy. "Uh . . ."

"The Duke is going to try to wind you up," said Just Alice. "Don't let him."

"Got it," said the boy. "And here I was worried she was going to be cross with me for having nothing to wear."

"Don't be ridiculous," whispered Just Alice. "She could hardly expect you to vagabond your way across the length of the Kingdoms and then turn up for dinner in doublet and silk hose."

13

The Duke turned up for dinner in doublet and silk hose. He also turned up in a watered silk shirt, a pair of shiny leather boots, a large gold medallion and a silver coronet. He sat at the head of a forty-man banquet table. Arrayed around the table was the answer to the mystery of what had become of so many of West Stanhope's knights. Dozens of them sat at the Duke's table, all in fine brocaded woolens and richly dyed leggings.

The Princess, as guest of honor, sat at the Duke's immediate right. Mennofar, Just Alice and the boy were seated halfway along the table, though Mennofar was obliged to stand on his chair just to see over the table. The rest of the table was filled out with the more senior men-at-arms.

When all the guests had taken their seats, the Duke stood to make a series of toasts. By tradition, the first toast went to the King. The second toast went to the Princess. When they had drunk that toast, the Duke said, "And I think, because of the special nature of the occasion, we should offer a third toast, this one for Her Highness's fiancé, uh . . ." He paused for a moment. "I'm so sorry, but it has slipped my mind. What are you called again?"

The boy colored as the entire company of men turned to look at him. "I haven't got a name, Your Grace," said the boy meekly.

"Nothing, eh?" said the Duke. He raised his goblet. "To nothing."

"To nothing," roared back the Duke's men, hoisting their goblets. At the far end of the table, a few of them tittered.

"Now, now," said the Duke. "None of that. Nothing is our guest." That inspired more laughter from the Duke's men.

The boy saw the Duke's eye fall on him, so he nodded in acknowledgment of the toast and ignored the insult.

Footmen brought out the first course. In front of each guest, they set a gelatin mold with the skeleton of a fish floating in it. The boy poked his with a fork. It wobbled a little.

"Fish aspic with intact skeleton," said the Duke. "A local specialty."

The Duke's men began wolfing theirs down with gusto.

"We don't get any meat, just the skeleton?" whispered the boy to Mennofar.

"The fish is soaked in lye and a special kind of broth that turns the flesh into gelatin," said Mennofar.

The boy poked the gelatin again. "That's the meat?" said the boy.

Mennofar nodded. He sliced off a big mouthful and swallowed it. "Ahh . . . delicious," he said. "And the bones just melt in your mouth."

"I think I'd rather have bat," said the boy.

Just Alice nodded and pushed hers toward the middle of the table.

When the Duke finished wolfing his down, he turned back to the boy. "I am well aware that softness is a virtue among women," he said. "But I have to wonder if it is possible for a woman to be too soft."

"I wouldn't know, Your Grace," said the boy. "You could ask a sage."

"I only ask as it would appear that your mother was so soft that she could not settle on a name for you," said the Duke. "Or perhaps she was too soft to remember?" Several of his men snickered like hyenas.

"Surely you would not ask a guest to speak ill of his own mother," said the Princess.

"No, no, idle ruminations only," said the Duke.

"I took no offense," said the boy, which earned him a little frown from the Duke.

"But what of your father? Did he not have some names to suggest to your mother?" said the Duke. "Or did he worry whether he knew her well enough to take the liberty?" That got some guffaws.

"I prove that he knew her very well," said the boy.

The table roared with laughter. The knight sitting next to the boy thumped him on the back and said, "Well said. Well said."

The Duke frowned. "Do forgive any insult," he said. "None was intended. I assumed your condition was unusual, but perhaps I am wrong. Perhaps I move in circles so rarefied that I don't even know what is common. Those of us at the top of society are frequently ignorant of the lives of the base." The laughter was scattered this time.

"You do yourself no justice," said the Princess. "The common and base are familiar enough, even in some more rarefied circles."

"How dare you!" hissed the Duke in a voice only the Princess could hear.

"You think I meant you?" asked the Princess, batting her eyes at him. "I can't think how you came to that conclusion."

The Duke spun on the boy and said, "Tell me, boy, what is the name of your tailor? I must ask him to work his magic on a garment or two of my own." Again, his men guffawed.

"Oh, I don't think you could afford my fiancé's tailor," said the Princess offhandedly.

This brought all conversation to a halt. The Duke turned to face her. "And just what do you mean by that?" he hissed. He waited a long time before adding, "Your Highness."

"When you failed to find any suitable clothing to lend to a weary traveler, I just assumed you were on the verge of bankruptcy yourself," said the Princess. "As I know that you would never willingly endure such a stain on your honor."

The Duke could not *admit* that he had deliberately insulted a guest. Through gritted teeth, he said, "Your Highness has seen right through me. Times are, indeed, tight until the next rents are due."

"What's that thing on the Duke's neck?" whispered Just Alice to the boy. She saw the mark when the Duke turned to talk to the Princess.

"I saw it when I was here before," whispered the boy back. "It's a tattoo or something. It looks familiar."

"It looks like the spade tip at the end of Ludwig's tail," whispered Just Alice.

The boy gasped, "You don't suppose that means—"

"So you two are just now realizing that Duke Geoffrey is the evil sorcerer who summoned the dragon?" whispered Mennofar.

"You knew?" whispered Just Alice.

"He's the only one with a motive," whispered Mennofar. "He lets a few would-be heroes get killed, rides in to save the day, marries the Princess and ensures his future claim to the throne."

"Or his rescue attempt fails and the Princess is killed. He looks like a hero for trying, gets to be the king anyway and is free to marry a richer princess," whispered the boy.

"That's a terrible thought," whispered Just Alice.

Mennofar, however, smiled at the boy. "That is goblin devious, that is," he whispered.

"What're you whispering about down there?" called out the Duke.

"Nothing, Your Grace," said the boy.

"Nothing? Or sweet nothings? It is unseemly for a young man promised to a princess to be whispering and giggling with a"—the Duke paused for emphasis—"peasant girl."

Although Just Alice more or less was a peasant, the Duke made it sound like a shameful secret. The boy jumped up and said, "You take that back."

"Alice may be a village girl, but she is also a dear friend. And my champion is true of heart. I see no cause for suspicion," said the Princess. Her tone was airy, but she looked worried.

The Duke smelled blood. He smiled and said, "I beg your pardon, Your Highness. I thought only of your honor."

"I may need a champion to protect me from the likes of dragons and wicked men, but against scurrilous rumor, I am quite capable of defending myself," said the Princess.

"Indeed?" said the Duke. Turning back to the boy, he said, "I hope you will forgive a little fatherly advice. Now, when the King grants you a title—Earl of Nothing, perhaps—you must set aside common pursuits, like carrying on with village girls." This was pretty rich, as it was well known there were few things the Duke liked more than carrying on with village girls.

Mennofar grabbed the boy's arm in a hopeless attempt to stop him. He was dragged along with the boy as the boy jumped up onto his chair. "You tried to kill the Princess," shouted the boy.

The dining hall fell completely silent.

"That would be treason," said the Duke, smiling. "A very serious accusation. I do hope you can prove it."

"That mark on your neck," said the boy. "It is the dragon's mark. Whoever bears the dragon's mark commands the dragon."

"Really?" said the Duke. "Having no knowledge of sorcery, I am unfamiliar with this tale. Where did you learn it?"

"The dragon said so," said Just Alice.

"It's true," said the Princess. "I heard it, too."

"At least we don't have to rely on the boy's word for that," said the Duke. "Did the dragon say I was the one who commanded him?"

"No," said the Princess.

"Or describe the mark?" said the Duke.

"Well . . . no," said the Princess.

"So someone, somewhere, bears a mark that may, or may not, look like the one on my neck and that allows him to command a dragon. Is that right?" said the Duke.

"Yes," said the Princess.

"And now you are your champion's champion," said the Duke. "How sweet. Well, I've a hundred men here who'll swear this is a birthmark that I've had all my life." A murmur went through the room as each man agreed that he would so swear. "So it seems to me that all you have is rumor and guesses."

"My father will be the judge of that," said the Princess.

"So he shall. So he shall," said the Duke. "But I shall judge another matter."

"What are you talking about?" said the Princess.

"A commoner has slanderously accused a nobleman and member of the royal family of treason, all in an effort to discredit that nobleman and possibly even have him wrongly put to death," said the Duke. He turned his gaze on the boy. "A most heinous and infamous crime. Remind me, what is the punishment for that?"

"I believe it is death by hanging, Your Grace," said the Majordomo.

The Duke slapped his forehead. "So it is," he said. "How could I have forgotten?"

"You are the spawn of the Foul One," whispered the Princess to the Duke.

"Such language, Your Highness," whispered the Duke back. Then he raised his voice so that all could hear. "Of course, I could be lenient. I could reduce his punishment to, say, having him branded and exiled. Oh, and some light torture, of course." The Duke glanced down at his fingernails. "I might be willing to do that . . . if you were to marry me instead."

"Never," said the Princess.

"And if you asked very nicely, I might even forgo the torture," said the Duke. "I could hardly refuse such a request from my fiancée on our engagement day. If she begged."

The Princess set her jaw.

"Very well," said the Duke. "Prepare the gallows."

"Save him!" urged Just Alice.

The Princess glanced back and forth between the Duke and the boy.

"I accept," said the Princess. "Now, let him go."

The Duke turned to the Majordomo. "Did that sound like begging to you?"

"No, Your Grace," said the Majordomo. "I don't think she got into the spirit of it."

"Quite right," said the Duke. "I would expect begging to be more . . ." He snapped his fingers, searching for the right word.

"Humiliating?" suggested the Majordomo.

The Duke smiled. "Yes, humiliating."

The Princess put her hands together and bowed her head. "Please," she said. A single tear ran down her cheek. "Please don't hurt him."

With one hand, the Duke lifted her chin. With the other, he gently wiped the tear from her cheek. "Anything for you, my love," he said. "Now, don't forget to thank me."

"Thank you, Your Grace," said the Princess.

The Duke accepted her thanks with a nod. Then he turned to his men and said, "Take the lot of them to the dungeon."

Guards grabbed Just Alice and the boy by the shoulders and pulled them from the table. Another lifted Mennofar into the air by his feet.

"No," cried the Princess. "You said you'd let them go unharmed. You promised."

"And so I shall, but not yet," said the Duke. "Do not think me such a great fool as to let them go until after we are wed."

The Princess wept as Just Alice, the boy and Mennofar were carried out of the room.

14

Tradition requires that a dungeon be cold, windowless and dank: a grim hole that robs the prisoners of all hope. The Duke was a great believer in tradition. The guards put the boy, Just Alice and Mennofar in leg chains, which they locked to great iron rings in the wall. Quite by chance, the Duke had several sets of manacles in various children's sizes, so the guards were able to lock Mennofar up as well. The three of them sat with their backs to the wall.

The boy looked down at Mennofar's ankles, which were already red and swollen. "Does it hurt badly?"

"It burns like fire, yes," said Mennofar. He smiled his pointy-toothed smile. "Thanks for asking."

The boy nodded. "You don't suppose there's any chance he really will let us go, do you?" There was a long pause. To fill the silence, the boy added, "I mean, once he's married the Princess, why would he care about us at all?"

"We know too much," said Just Alice. "He'll make a big show of exiling us, but our escort will kill us as soon as we're out of sight."

"I was hoping I was wrong about that," said the boy. "Still, something will stop him, right? I mean, it's not his fate to be king, so he's bound to fail."

"Unless it *is* his fate to be king," said Just Alice. "He's the closest male relative to the King. What if by trying to put Princess Alice on the throne, King Julian is the one battling fate? By your lights, it'd be King Julian who's bound to fail, while the Duke's bound to succeed, right?"

Just Alice was very good at turning things backward. There was no denying that what she said was right, but it seemed wrong that a man like Geoffrey should be fated to be a king. Only fate did not work this way. It wasn't about right or wrong. The Three Sisters just drew each fate by lot. It might be Geoffrey's lot to be king, or it might not. There was no way to know. That was the trouble with fate. When you were sure what everyone's fate was, everything worked nicely. When you were not, things got confusing fast.

"Maybe we could just escape," said the boy.

"How?" said Just Alice.

"I don't know," said the boy. "Mennofar? Can you help?"

"It would please me greatly to give that guard a bite he would not soon forget," said Mennofar.

"No, I mean, can't you use your vision to see a way out of this mess?" said the boy. "To find some way to escape?"

"What, and ruin all the fun?" said Mennofar.

"You've got a strange sense of fun," said Just Alice.

Mennofar only smiled in response.

The boy put his arm around her shoulder, and they huddled together against the cold. "We'll figure something out," he said. He wished he believed it.

♠

Pennants snapped in the breeze. Horses snorted and pawed the ground. Men grumbled about the early hour. Then the horn sounded. The great wooden wheels of the supply wagons creaked as they began to turn. The men-at-arms fell into a marching column. The Duke's army slowly made its way west down the Stanhope Road.

The Duke was taking the Princess to Farnham to request the King's consent to their marriage. He was bringing all of his knights and all of his men-at-arms to help the King put this request in context. Large bodies of armed men often proved useful when it came to putting matters in context.

To help the Princess keep matters in context, the Duke brought the boy, Just Alice and Mennofar. The three of them, still shackled, were thrown onto the back of one of the wagons. Several guards rode with them, so they could not talk freely. The boy spent the long, bone-jarring ride watching the countryside slowly change from empty wasteland to snug little farms. He wondered what had become of his great fate. It had never seemed further away.

♠

Oswald the Sage lived at the very edge of town. So when the Duke's company came to Middlebury, his was the first stoop they marched past. Another man, one not driven wild with worry about the fate of his only child, might have shown more caution when an unfamiliar army turned up on his doorstep. He might have snuck out the back or hidden his money under that one loose floorboard or even just stayed inside, pretending not to be home. Oswald, however, charged out of his house and accosted the nearest soldier.

"Is there news of the dragon?" he said. "He has my daughter as well as the Princess."

"Go away," said the soldier, and pushed him aside.

Oswald grabbed the arm of another soldier. "Please, any news. Anything at all."

"Shove off," said the second soldier. He yanked his arm away and trudged on.

Oswald looked up across the ranks of men and saw the Duke. "Your Grace!" he cried. He elbowed his way through the men toward the Duke. "Your Grace, I am looking for news of my daughter. She was taken by the dragon."

From atop his charger, the Duke looked down at Oswald. "Who is this old fool?" he said to one of his lieutenants.

"I expect he's the village idiot or something," said the lieutenant.

"Then give him a thumping and send him on his way," said the Duke. He waved his hand in dismissal.

Oswald saw the wagon with Just Alice and the boy in chains. His heart filled with joy and horror at the same time. She had been saved from the dragon only to be delivered up to the Duke. "No, please, Your Grace," said Oswald. "My daughter's a good girl. Please let her go."

The Duke stopped his horse. He pointed to Just Alice and said, "You're this girl's father?"

"Yes, Your Grace," said Oswald. "But whatever she's accused of, it can't be true. She's a dutiful girl who knows her place." This wasn't entirely true, but it didn't seem like the right moment for the truth.

"Seize him," said the Duke. "The girl will make less trouble if we have her father."

The Duke's men grabbed Oswald, slapped him in irons and dumped him into the back of the wagon.

♠

Elsewhere in Middlebury, the unexpected arrival of a large group of heavily armed men quite naturally set off alarms. The town's few defenders were badly outnumbered. The Earl rubbed his temples vigorously. The dragon was bad enough. If Middlebury was overrun, he would be a laughingstock. There was a good chance he would also be dead. But people would still laugh at him.

He rode out to meet the company and challenge its commander to personal combat. Given his age, the Earl did not care for his chances, but he had to do something. He found the company out on the edge of town, and issued his challenge. "Who goes there? Be you friend of Middlebury or—" When he saw the Princess, he vaulted from his saddle and knelt before her with surprising speed and grace. "Your Highness, how it gladdens me to see you safely delivered from the evil clutches of the foul beast."

Princess Alice glanced back at Duke Geoffrey, her face filled with fear.

"I take it you mean the dragon," said Duke Geoffrey.

"Your Grace, greetings be upon you," said the Earl. "I certainly hope I meant the dragon. Pray tell me there are no other foul beasts preying upon our poor kingdom."

"No foul beasts at all, for the dragon has been defeated and driven from the land," said Duke Geoffrey. He smiled broadly. "And more joy still, Princess Alice has most generously agreed to be my wife."

"Has she?" said the Earl, glancing uneasily at the size of the Duke's company. "Why then, congratulations, Your Grace." To Princess Alice, he added, "And best of luck to you, Your Highness."

The Duke pursed his lips. "Best wishes," he said. "One traditionally offers best wishes to the bride."

"Oh, dear," said the Earl. For some reason, the Duke had taken Oswald the Sage and his daughter, Alice, prisoner. Even more unlikely, the Earl's own Magan hung from the side of the wagon they were shackled in. The Earl carefully avoided looking in their direction. "What did I say?"

"You said 'best of luck.' "

"Did I? I'm afraid I've gotten a little foggy with age," said the Earl. Out of the corner of his eye, the Earl studied Magan. There were several new dents in her, along with two strange crunched-in bits along the edge. The paint was chipped and scratched all over, nearly half gone. The Earl wondered if someone had gone sledding on her. "Please do forgive me."

"Of course I forgive you," said Princess Alice.

"Yes, we forgive you," said Duke Geoffrey. "And as proof, let me invite you to join us as we ride to Farnham to seek the King's blessing."

"A generous invitation," said the Earl. "Most kind, indeed, but travel is hard and, as I said, I am an old man."

Duke Geoffrey leaned forward in his saddle. His smile vanished. "You're quite sure you won't come?"

"My wife is doing poorly. I should not leave her side," said the Earl. "I must decline."

"That saddens me," said the Duke.

"Surely you have but to look to your radiant bride and all care will melt away," said the Earl. "Now, if you will excuse me, I must return to my wife." Without waiting for a response, the Earl jumped back onto his horse and rode off. The Earl might have been an old man, but he was not an old fool. The size of Duke Geoffrey's body of men, Oswald and his daughter taken hostage, his own Magan seized and, most especially, the look of fear in Princess Alice's eyes—the Earl knew what all of it meant: he had to beat Duke Geoffrey to Farnham.

He rode toward his castle until he was out of the Duke's sight. Then he turned down a series of side alleys and rode around the back of the market. At the edge of town, he took the foot trail that ran toward the old mill. After a few miles, he came to the low stone wall that marked the far side of Evan the Broad's cow fields. Judging that he had gone far enough, he followed the wall north to where it met the Stanhope Road.

Horses gallop faster than men in armor march, so the Earl had a lead on the Duke despite taking the back way. Just how much of a lead, however, he had no way of knowing. Hard as it might be on a man his age, the Earl thundered down the road as though the Foul One himself rode at his heels.

♠

The great ship lay snug in her berth in Farnham's harbor. A long line of porters carried crate after crate down the gangplank. Casimir stood on the deck and watched them with satisfaction. Then one of them stumbled and nearly lost his footing. A large wooden crate pitched forward wildly and began to slip off his back. With a mighty grunt, the porter righted both himself and the crate. The porter was a brawny man.

"Be careful, you oaf," Casimir called down at him. "Those silks are worth ten of you."

The porter squinted up at Casimir for a moment before letting go of the crate. It dropped to the pier with an almighty crash. "Sorry, sir," said the porter. "It slipped." He jumped down onto the pier and joined the crowd of porters waiting to come back up onto the ship.

"You did that on purpose!" shouted Casimir. "Curse you! I'll report you to the harbormaster! I'll have you flogged! I'll—" But it was too late. As soon as the porter joined his fellows, Casimir lost track of him. Stanhopers were all pale as ghosts; they all looked alike. Maybe the harbormaster would agree to flog the whole lot of them.

Casimir spun on his heel and found himself face to face with the Factor. "Where've you been?"

"Sorry, sir," said the Factor. "I was indisposed." He did look a little green.

"Wanted to squeeze one last sick out of the trip, eh?" said Casimir.

"I wouldn't say that I regret our arrival," said the Factor. He gazed out over the rooftops of Farnham. "And it does look like a pleasant little *village*."

"Opportunities never *look* promising," said Casimir. "If they did, someone would have snapped them up already."

"I'm quite sure you're right," said the Factor in a tone that suggested just the opposite.

"Hang your lip," said Casimir. "Now, keep an eye on these stumblefoots. They'll drop my cargo in the ocean if they can get away with it. Little men always want to take their betters down a notch."

When Just Alice and Oswald were reunited, they cried and kissed each other on the cheek. They also tried to hug, but the chains made that impossible. Oswald said how worried he had been. Just Alice took this the wrong way, so she pointed out that Oswald's getting himself taken hostage meant that she would now have him to worry about. And when Oswald looked a little hurt by her saying so, they had to cry and kiss and fail to hug each other again.

Once it started to get dark, the Duke's company made camp on the side of the road. The boy, Just Alice, Oswald and Mennofar were allowed down off the wagon, but their shackles were still attached to it by a length of chain. The wagon itself took six oxen to move. There was no hope that the four of them would be able to shift it even a little.

Dinner was just bread and a scoop of beans. While they ate, a nearby group of soldiers built up a great fire. One of the guards nudged another and pointed. Around the fire, the soldiers were passing wineskins. One after another, the guards got up to join the soldiers. When only one guard was left, he checked the shackles of the four prisoners before joining the other guards and soldiers around the fire.

"What happened?" said Oswald once he was gone.

With a few interruptions from the boy, Just Alice told Oswald the story of her rescue, the Princess's rescue and the Duke's treachery.

When she was done, Oswald simply nodded. He thought for a long moment and said to the boy, "Son, the debt that I owe you is one that can never be repaid. If ever there is any service I can perform for you, you have but to name it."

"Thank you, sir," said the boy. "Maybe you could think of a way to escape?"

Oswald stroked his beard a moment. "That might be a little too . . . *practical* for a sage," he said. "Perhaps your goblin friend could help—"

"Do not insult me, sir," said Mennofar.

"And it's no good me asking him if this scheme or that plan can work," said the boy. "He'll just say yes, because it's the future, and very nearly everything is possible."

Mennofar smiled his pointy-toothed smile.

"I see. I see," said Oswald. He leaned in and whispered, "Still, I'm pretty sure we'll be rescued soon."

Just Alice leaned in, too. "What? How?"

"The Earl saw right through the Duke," said Oswald. "I'm sure of it. You saw how he acted."

"I thought that was because his wife was sick," said Just Alice. "Why am I the only one who misses these things?"

"I missed it, too," said the boy, earning himself a smile from Just Alice. "Besides, so what if he did?"

"He'll be riding to Farnham to warn the King," said Oswald. "And the King will send the army to rescue us."

"Rescue the Princess, anyway," said Just Alice.

"We'll be rescued along the way," said Oswald. "You can stake your life on it."

"We do not have much choice in the matter," said Mennofar.

That thought stopped the conversation dead. Everyone sat in silence for a moment, staring into the inky dark of the night sky. Finally, Just Alice said, "Papa might be able to help free you in another way."

"What other way?" said the boy. He rattled his chains at her.

Mennofar grumbled a little.

"Papa is a terribly clever man, and he knows all kinds of things," said Just Alice. "He's a fully qualified sage." In the dark, she slid her hand into the boy's. "And he can be trusted with a secret."

"Yes, of course," said Oswald. "Whatever this matter is, you may rest assured that I will never reveal it."

The boy hesitated.

"Do you want me to tell him?" said Just Alice.

"No," said the boy, and he told Oswald his story, from the murder of Tibor to the day the two of them met.

When he was done, Oswald said, "Well, that is quite a story."

The boy nodded.

"And you, sir?" said Oswald to Mennofar. "You still will not simply reveal the truth?"

"My honor as a goblin forbids it," said Mennofar. He smiled toothily.

"Very well," said Oswald. "To sum up, for as long as you can remember you have been held as a slave by this man Casimir—do interrupt me if I get something wrong—and what we know from Mennofar's answers is that you were not born free nor were you freed. And finally, we know from his answers that you are not a slave, is that right?"

"Yes," said the boy. "The problem is how to prove it. Maybe some obscure point of law or—"

"Based only on what you have told me," said Oswald

with great drama, "I already know that one of the answers Mennofar has given is false."

"An outrageous suggestion," said Mennofar.

"Really?" said the boy. "Which one?"

"Oh, I haven't the foggiest idea," said Oswald, stroking his beard.

It was too much. "How? How?" said the boy. "How can you know one is false if you don't know which one?" Tears filled the boy's eyes.

Oswald patted him awkwardly on the shoulder. "I didn't mean to upset you," he said. "I know it by logic. If several things, taken together, lead to a contradiction, then at least one must be false. Here, everything we know says that you both are and are not a slave. That is not possible. Therefore, at least one of the things we know is false."

The boy looked at him expectantly.

"Unfortunately, logic cannot tell us which one," said Oswald.

"Well, then logic can go hang," said the boy. "What else have you got?"

Oswald said nothing.

"Well?" said the boy angrily. "What is it? Am I a slave? Is that it?"

"Yes," said Mennofar.

"No fair. That wasn't one of my questions," said the boy. "I was talking to— Wait, what did you say?"

"I said yes," said Mennofar. "By all the laws of the Kingdoms, you are a slave."

15

"A slave?" said the boy. "How can I be a slave?"

Mennofar put a sad expression on his face. "It is with some regret," he said, "that I will be obliged to ask that you put that request to me in the form of a yes-or-no question, or, perhaps more realistically, a series of yes-or-no—"

"Mennofar!" snapped Just Alice.

"All right, all right," said Mennofar. He turned to the boy. "Your mother's name was Reka, and she was born to a peasant family in High Albemarle. One year, there was a drought, and the crops failed. When his tenants could not pay their rents, the Count of Mossglum took one child from each family instead. Reka was sold to Casimir and grew up a slave in his household.

"Your father's name was Kelemen, and his people were vassals of the Duke of Esterly. The Duke tried to overthrow the King of High Albemarle. He pressed all of his vassals into a great army and met the King's forces in battle. The Duke was defeated and hanged. His soldiers were all sold into slavery.

"Kelemen, along with many others, was put to work loading and unloading Casimir's ships. Reka's duties included cooking for the dock slaves. She grew fond of Kelemen and slipped him extra food, little treats, that sort of thing. Eventually, um . . . er . . . well, in the way these things happen, you came along," said Mennofar. "Your mother was a slave, your father was a slave, and so, by law, are you."

"What happened to Reka and Kelemen?" said Just Alice.

"And what about my father's ring?" said the boy. "If he was nothing but a slave, where did it come from?"

"Not long before you were born, Casimir sold a great many of his slaves, including Kelemen," said Mennofar. "Reka and Kelemen did not want to lose each other, and they did not want you to be born into slavery. So Reka stole a hammer and snuck into the warehouse where

Kelemen and the others were chained up, waiting for the ship that would take them away. They used the hammer to break his chain and escape. But they were caught before they made it out of Albemarle City. Kelemen was hanged on the spot, but Casimir wanted something back on the loss of two slaves. They waited until after you were born to hang Reka. Your ring is the link of chain Reka and Kelemen broke to escape."

"You told me I was supposed to be free," said the boy. His mind raced and he had trouble catching his breath. The image of Tibor's body with one eye pointed slackly down came to the boy's mind for the first time in months. Even though he had known what Rodrigo was going to do, he had just closed his eyes. Doing the utmost to save his master was the duty of every slave, but he had done nothing to save Tibor. When Mennofar had told him he was not a slave, he had let himself think he was off the hook for that. Now that he knew better, a clutch closed in around his heart.

"I wish things were different," said Mennofar, and he even turned a little darker to prove how sad he was.

"You tricked me," said the boy. One by one, the Ninety-Nine Duties of a Slave marched through his head. He had violated nearly all of them. He had even let himself feel hatred for his master. He turned away to hide the tears forming in his eyes. "I turned renegade because of you. I defied the will of my master—of the gods."

"No need to give me so much credit as that," said Mennofar. "You ran away all on your own. Before we ever met."

And it was true. "You're right," said the boy. "I only believed you because I wanted it to be true." The boy sank even lower. He had defied his fate and denied Casimir his due. He knew there would be a price to pay for such selfishness. His gut went soft at the thought of burning in the fire and serving the Foul One in the Pit. Forever.

"Hang on," said Just Alice. "You can't be both a slave and not a slave, can you?"

"No," admitted the boy.

Mennofar smiled. His skin turned a rich emerald green.

"So are you sure he really told you that you weren't?" said Just Alice.

"Of course," said the boy.

"But how did he tell you?" said Just Alice. "What words did he use?"

"I said, 'Am I really a slave?' " said the boy. "And he said no."

"Mennofar?" said Just Alice.

Smiling even more broadly, Mennofar shook his head.

Just Alice looked straight into the boy's eyes. "What, precisely, was the question you asked him?"

"Um," said the boy. "Uh . . ." He racked his brain,

but it was hard to think with Just Alice's gaze boring into him.

"The question, precisely as put to me," said Mennofar, "was, 'Am I truly and justly a slave?' "

"See, I told you," said the boy, relieved that he had not remembered it wrong.

"You idiot!" said Just Alice. "You knot-headed, soup-for-brains, thickwit numskull." If not for her chains, she surely would have smacked him. " 'Am I truly and justly a slave?' That was your question?"

"Yes. So what?"

"I believe Alice's concern is that the way you asked the question may have caused some confusion," said Oswald.

"It's a compound question," said Just Alice. "He could say no if any part of it was false."

"So?" said the boy.

"So, what if you were truly a slave but not justly one?" said Just Alice.

"That's stupid," said the boy. "How could I be one and not the other? That makes no sense at all."

"You're quite sure about that, are you?" said Just Alice.

"My father was captured in wartime," said the boy, "and my mother was sold to pay her family's debts, so I was born a slave. That's where slaves come from." The boy stopped and thought about what he had just said. No one spoke for a long moment. "If I am not justly a slave, then who is?"

"I have my standards," said Mennofar. "I will not answer that question."

"I can never get anywhere with you," said the boy. "Every time I get one thing from you, you turn it right back around again. Do you enjoy torturing me?"

"Yes," said Mennofar.

"That might be the only true thing you've ever said to me," said the boy. "I'm finished with you. I've got nothing more to ask."

"Is anyone justly a slave?" said Just Alice.

"Don't you start in," said the boy.

"No, that's what you should ask him," said Just Alice. "Is anyone justly a slave?"

"Don't be ridiculous," said the boy.

"Just ask," said Just Alice.

"Fine," said the boy. "Mennofar, is anyone justly a slave?"

"No," said Mennofar. The boy gawped at him.

"Well, that ties it up rather neatly, then," said Oswald. "Although it means you're a slave after all." He thought about this a moment more. "Oh, dear."

The boy, however, was still gawping at Mennofar. "How can you say that?" he asked. "How can that be?"

"Makes sense to me," said Just Alice. "Why should your poor father be a slave just because some nobleman lost a battle to some other nobleman? And it's even worse for your mother. The crops fail, so she has to be a slave? That's hardly fair, is it?"

"It is unjust for one man to own another," said Mennofar.

"Exactly," said Just Alice. "Come to think of it, why should one man be king and another be a peasant?"

"Let's watch that kind of talk," said Oswald. He glanced around as if the Captain of the Guard might be lurking behind a shrub somewhere.

"But it's fated to be," said the boy.

"There is no fate," said Mennofar.

"I could have told you that," said Just Alice. "In fact, I did, didn't I?"

"You're wrong!" said the boy. "Every man has a fate. As we are born, the Three Sisters draw it from the great bowl."

"My vision shows me otherwise," said Mennofar.

"But how can you know that?" said the boy. "Ha! You're not going to trick me again. You cannot see the gods, not even with your third eye. You told me so yourself."

"A good point," said Oswald. "Well reasoned."

"When I look into the future," said Mennofar, "I can see the endlessly unfolding possibilities it holds, the immense number of paths that a single life can take. When I see these possibilities, all the things that might happen, I know that the gods have not fixed a single unerring, unchanging destiny for each person."

"Well, maybe not every little detail is set in stone," said the boy, "but a person's life is what it is. It's not like I could ever become King of High Albemarle."

Mennofar closed his eyes and concentrated hard. When he opened them, he smiled, flashing his many pointed teeth. "It is unlikely," he said. "But not impossible."

This was a bit much, even for Just Alice. "How?" she asked.

"All he has to do is escape the Duke, return to High Albemarle and lead a slave rebellion," said Mennofar. "It would almost certainly end in failure and death, but if the rebels won, he could wind up being king."

"Really?" said the boy. His prospects were looking up.

"Of course, if you really want to be a king, West Stanhope is a much safer play. All you have to do is foil the Duke and ask for Princess Alice's hand in marriage as your reward for rescuing her," said Mennofar.

"That does make sense," said Oswald. "When she ascends to the throne, you'd be prince consort . . . or captain regent . . . or something like that."

Mennofar nodded while Just Alice glared at Oswald. The boy was too deep in his own thoughts to notice. Having a fate meant knowing where he belonged, even if where he belonged was at the bottom. With a fate, he knew what he was supposed to be and what he was supposed to do. It was a comfort. Even when he lost his fate, he still knew what to do: go and find it. But if the gods had not set his fate when he was born, then there was no reason for any of the things that had happened to him or

Reka or Kelemen. Or even Rodrigo. Without fate, there might be nothing at all. Belief in it explained everything.

Except that it did not. Fate was a reason, but it was a terrible one. Fate said that his mother and father should die because they did not want their child to live a life of endless drudgery. Fate said that Rodrigo should never see his daughter because Tibor thought it might be inconvenient.

He had changed. It was that simple. While he searched for what he thought was his fate, he had been forced to act as though he had none. He had made his own choices without regard for who he was supposed to be. For the first time, he had lived with doubt and uncertainty. Not knowing meant exploring and discovering. Yes, it was frightening, but it was also fun. Some of his choices were wise, and some were foolish, but all were his and his alone. Once he had thought fate was an anchor, holding him steady, giving him a place in the world. Now he saw that it was a shackle, binding him in place. Except that he was held prisoner not by iron bonds but by his own belief. When he let that go, the shackle simply vanished.

At least, the ones in his head did. The ones used to chain him up were still there. The boy stared down at them for a moment. "At least one good thing comes of this," he said, turning to Alice. "You solved a goblin's puzzle. If we survive, you can get your extraordinary from the Council of Sages."

Just Alice rolled her eyes back up into her head. "No, I can't," she said.

"But it's a goblin's puzzle," said the boy. "You said solving one of those—"

"It'd mean telling people you're a slave," said Just Alice. "You'd be sent back to High Albemarle."

"Oh, right," said the boy.

"Look on the bright side," said Mennofar. "The Duke may have us all executed and save you worrying about any of this."

♠

The Earl rode hard, and the Earl rode long. He rode until every single part of him ached, even the parts he'd forgotten he had. Even so, when he pulled his horse to a stop in front of the royal palace, he was, at best, only a few hours ahead of the Duke's company. He vaulted from his saddle and strode dramatically through the palace gates. At least, he would have, if his legs had not given out as soon as he touched the ground. Fortunately, the palace guardsmen saw him stumble. Two of them propped him up.

"Lord Middlebury," said one. "Are you all right?"

"No time, no time," said the Earl. "You"—he pointed to the first—"find the Captain of the Guard and take him to the King. And you"—he pointed to the other—"see to my horse."

"Yes, my lord," they said in unison. Ordering people around and having them say, "Yes, my lord," was one of the few perks of being an earl.

"Now I must go to the King," said the Earl. It was mostly for his own benefit, as he did not want to fail when he was so close. He set off through the palace gates at what could best be described as a brisk shuffle.

♠

The cabinet was deep in the throes of another meeting when the doors of the library flew open with a bang. Every head snapped up. The pale and sweating Earl staggered into the room.

The Bailiff was the first to recover from the surprise. He jumped up and said, "Your Majesty, may I present Your Right Trusty and Well-Beloved Cousin, the—" It was as far as he got before the Earl fainted dead away.

"Godric!" cried the King, and he rushed to the Earl's side. "Are you all right?"

The Earl's eyes fluttered open. He said, "Your Majesty—"

"Don't overtax yourself," said the King. He pointed at one of the footmen. "Bring food and drink."

"Your Majesty," said the Earl. "It's the Princess."

"You have news?" said the King. "She lives?"

"She lives," said the Earl. "The dragon is gone."

"Let us give praise to the gods," said the King.

"Not yet," said the Earl. He sat up. "Duke Geoffrey has her. He forced her to agree to marry him. Even now he rides here to seek your permission."

"Has he lost his mind!" cried the Bailiff.

Everyone turned and stared at the Bailiff.

"I beg your pardon, Your Highness," said the Bailiff, bowing deeply. "The moment got the better of me."

The King nodded. "Think nothing of it," he said. "And you're right. I will never consent to this. Even Geoffrey must know that."

"Which is why he brings a great host of men with him," said the Earl.

"Marching an army on the capital?" said the Tipstaff. "That's almost treason."

"The arrogance of the man," said the Seneschal.

"Geoffrey has troubled this land for long enough," said the King. "We will take the field against him and put an end to his mischief, once and for all."

"A fine plan, Your Highness," said the Captain of the Guard. After a pause, he added, "Perhaps His Lordship could let us know just how big a host we are talking about?"

"A phalanx of knights and a full company of men-at-arms," said the Earl. "Maybe a few more."

The Captain of the Guard winced a little. "As many as that?" he said.

"We have the men to defeat such a force," said the King. "Surely."

"Of course," said the Captain of the Guard. "Except that most of your knights and men-at-arms are off searching for the Princess." He looked down at the floor. "I'm afraid Duke Geoffrey has picked his moment rather well."

"Your Highness, I can rally your troops," said the Earl. "Let me ride forth and reassemble your forces." Godric sat up and felt a little dizzy.

"Good man, Godric," said the King, and he thumped the Earl on the back. "We'll bar the gates and make ready for a siege. When Godric has put the army back together, he can relieve us." He turned to the Captain of the Guard. "How long can we hold out?"

"We should be able to—"

"Your Majesty," said the Chamberlain. "I fear that we may be acting with undue haste. We have not examined the full ramifications of—"

"We don't have time for one of your committees!" said the King.

"He'll kill her!" said the Chamberlain. Everyone's head spun to stare at him. "If we bar the gates, he'll kill the Princess."

"He wouldn't," said the King.

"He would," said the Chamberlain. "Without hesitation."

"But he wants to marry her," said the King.

"He does not," said the Chamberlain. "He wants the appearance of legitimacy that comes from marrying her with your blessing. That is her only value to him. If you declare him a rebel and an outlaw—"

"He is a rebel and an outlaw," said the King.

"Yes, but if you *declare* him one, he loses all reason to pretend he is not," said the Chamberlain. "He will kill the Princess, storm the walls, hang us all and probably burn the city for good measure. That way, he still gets to be king."

"None of that will make him the rightful King of West Stanhope," said the King.

"And anyone who says *that* will also be hanged," said the Chamberlain.

The other members of the cabinet carefully avoided the King's eye.

"Then, what would you have me do?" said the King.

"Open the gates to the city," said the Chamberlain. "Bless the marriage."

"You're saying we let him win," said the King.

"I'm saying he already has," said the Chamberlain.

The King sank back heavily into his chair. "May the gods preserve us."

16

As the Duke's army marched west, the people of West Stanhope fled before them. Fields were abandoned in the middle of plowing. Villages stood empty and lifeless. Every inn had its shutters and doors nailed closed. Oswald, Just Alice and the boy reassured one another that the King's men were bound to be around the next bend or over the next rise, waiting to surprise the Duke's army. But when they rounded every turn and topped every hill, all they saw was more road and more empty countryside. No rescuers ever appeared. For his part, all Mennofar did was smile.

Late in the morning of the third day, the Duke's army crested the final hill. The great plain that sloped gently down to Farnham was empty. The city gates stood wide open. It was finally clear that the King was not going to take the field.

The army came to a halt long enough for the four prisoners to be brought before the Duke. The Duke sat atop his great black charger, with the Princess next to him on a pure white mare. He studied the four of them through narrowed eyes. "Unchain them," he said.

"Your Grace?" said the Majordomo in surprise.

"Appearances must be maintained," said the Duke. "This is supposed to be a happy occasion, is it not?"

"Very true," said the Majordomo, bowing slightly. He turned and snapped his fingers at the guards. "You heard His Grace. Unchain them!"

While their shackles were being removed, the Duke turned to the Princess. "You have promised to be my bride, Your Highness," he said.

The Princess nodded.

"Renege and they will be the ones to pay the price."

She glanced at the prisoners and nodded again.

The Duke turned back to the Majordomo. "I want two men guarding each prisoner. If anyone tries to escape, kill them all." He pointed at Just Alice and smiled. "And start with the girl."

♠

First went the knights, all in a long column. As each one rode through the city gates, he dipped his lance so as not to knock the tip against the keystone. Next came a column of men-at-arms, marching four abreast into the city. Oswald, Just Alice, the boy and Mennofar, along with their guards, followed them. And right after them rode the Duke, with the Princess beside him. Finally, there was another column of the Duke's men-at-arms, this one a good bit rowdier than the first.

News of the Princess's return spread like wildfire, and great crowds of people lined the streets to see if it was really true. When they saw the Princess riding by the Duke's side, many whispered, "Her Highness's hand, that's what he'll be asking for." "Don't see how His Majesty can refuse," others muttered back. A few people cheered, but mostly the Duke's men marched by silent crowds. The Duke waved and smiled as if the crowds roared in approval.

They marched through the city and into the courtyard of the royal palace. There, the royal household stood ready to receive them. There were trumpeters and a six-man honor guard. The King and Queen stood next to the Earl of Middlebury and all the members of the cabinet. Everyone was lined up by wig size, right up to the King, whose hairpiece was held aloft by two of the burlier footmen.

Everything was prepared for a formal ceremony, but before the honor guard could raise their swords in salute, even before the trumpeters could sound the fanfare, the Princess cried out, "Mama! Papa!" She leapt from her saddle and ran straight into their arms. The King and Queen swept her up and wept openly.

"I was sick with worry for you," said the Queen.

"I was very frightened," said the Princess, "but you must—"

"She's safe and sound now," said the King.

"Yes, and we must have a great banquet to celebrate," said the Queen.

The Duke cleared his throat.

With great reluctance, the King looked up at the Duke. "Goodness, do forgive us, Your Grace."

The Duke smiled tightly. "Not at all," he said. "Naturally, it's a very sentimental occasion." He took his feet from his stirrups and turned to dismount. The Chamberlain waved on the trumpeters. When they sounded the fanfare, the Duke's horse started in surprise and dumped him face-first onto the ground. Clenching his teeth, he stood and dusted himself off. When he was done, he bowed deeply and said, "Your Majesty, it gives me great personal pleasure to return to your care the Princess Alice, unharmed."

"Yes, and we are eternally grateful to you for that," said the King.

"And your gratitude is more precious than gold," said the Duke. "But as I, personally, saved her from the ferocious dragon—"

"What?!" exclaimed the Princess.

"*I* rescued Her Highness from the dragon," said the Duke, never looking away from the King. "As soon as I heard of Her Highness's distress, I rode out from my castle and confronted the beast. With no thought for my own safety, I courageously engaged the vile worm in personal combat. And when I single-handedly defeated it, it fled the kingdom, never to be seen again."

"And that's exactly how it happened?" said the King.

"At least a hundred of these men will swear to it," said the Duke. "So, that's exactly how it happened."

Behind the Duke, the Princess shook her head just a little.

The King looked to the Princess. "Sweetheart, do you have anything to say?" he asked.

The Princess looked back at the Duke's men. "No, Papa," she said.

The boy shifted back and forth from one foot to the other. The Duke was going to have his way because no one dared tell the truth about him. "He's lying!" shouted the boy. His startled guard reached out to grab him, but the boy dodged the man's grasp.

"Who dares?" said the Duke.

"Don't," said Just Alice. "He'll kill you."

She was right, but the Duke was going to kill them anyway. The boy slipped through a gap in the crowd. His guard came after him, but the gap was too narrow for a full-grown man.

The boy wormed out of the front of the crowd and shouted, "The Duke is lying!"

The Duke glared at the boy.

The guard burst out of the crowd behind the boy, but when he caught sight of the Duke's glare, he stepped right back into the crowd again.

The boy darted up to the King. Unsure what else to do, he went down on his hands and knees and pressed his forehead to the ground.

"Nice to see a young man who knows how to grovel properly," said the Chamberlain to the Seneschal.

"So few do nowadays," said the Seneschal.

"Please forgive me for interrupting, Your Majesty," said the boy, "but the Duke is lying to you. He didn't rescue Princess Alice from the dragon. I did."

"Pay no attention to this absurd ragamuffin," said the Duke. "He's out of his mind."

"I am not," said the boy. "The Duke didn't need to rescue her from the dragon because he used black magic to summon the dragon. He made the dragon kidnap the Princess so he could force you to let him marry her."

"Preposterous on its face," said the Duke. He snapped his fingers at a couple of his men-at-arms. They moved toward the boy.

"I cannot take such a serious accusation lightly," said the King.

"Nor should you, Your Majesty," said the Duke. "Let me put this matter to rest. I give you my word as a gentleman and as a peer of the realm and as a member of the royal family—and, I might add, as a leader of many, *many* men—that his wild accusations are without basis." He bowed a little toward the King. "You will, I hope, take my word over that of a nameless guttersnipe."

The King looked out over the Duke's men and sighed. "I suppose I must," he said.

"I thank you for clearing my name of this vile slander," said the Duke. He smiled venomously at the boy. "You will also, I hope, mete out an appropriate punishment for this heinous crime."

"Must we?" said the King.

"Oh, yes," said the Duke. "The boy must hang."

It was all a joke, only one with a punch line the boy did not like. Nothing he could say would change anything. So long as the Duke had his men, the truth did not matter. He could say whatever he wanted, and the King would pretend to believe him. Everyone else would go along with the sham for the same reason. Being surrounded by his men gave the Duke power over truth. And whoever held power over truth could remake the world, even if only for a time.

What the boy needed was a little of that power for himself—a claim that the Duke had no way to contradict. He threw back his head and looked all the way down his nose, just as the Duke had. "I am now prepared to reveal my true identity," he said in as lordly a tone as he could manage. "I am Rodrigo Tibor Casimir, the Count of Mossglum in the Kingdom of High Albemarle."

Everyone stared at the boy.

"You're a . . . count?" said the Majordomo.

"Every son of the noble House of Mossglum takes a holy vow to spend a year and a day wandering the earth in impoverished anonymity," said the boy. "By pure chance, my year and a day ended this very moment."

"That's—that's preposterous," said the Duke, which, to be fair, it was.

"Your Grace should be more generous to our guest," said the Princess. She stood next to the boy. "Eastern customs may strike us as exotic, but to call them preposterous is simply unkind."

The Duke glared at the Princess in hateful wonder. "Your Highness misunderstands me—"

"My Lord of Mossglum," said the King, "as King of West Stanhope, I recognize you as a foreign nobleman and welcome you to our kingdom."

The Duke said, "Your Majesty cannot seriously propose to—" He paused, and his cobra smile returned. "Very well, as I have been slandered not by a common guttersnipe who can be summarily hanged, but by a nobleman and guest of the King, I demand that my honor be satisfied in that most ancient and traditional manner."

The boy looked at the Duke. If the Duke liked it, it could not be anything good.

"On the field of honor," said the Duke.

"He means a duel," said Mennofar, who had slipped out of the crowd to join the boy.

"Do you accept?" asked the Duke.

The Duke was twice the boy's age, stood more than a foot taller and outweighed him by a hundred pounds. "I don't have a choice, do I?" said the boy.

"Not if you're really a count," said the Duke. "Bring the boy's—excuse me, the Lord of Mossglum's—arms and armor." The Duke's men sniggered.

One of the Duke's men came forward carrying Magan.

"That's it?" said the Duke. "No sword? No lance?"

"No, Your Grace," said the guard.

The Duke looked down his long nose at the boy. "I suppose you just faced the dragon bare-handed, then?"

"Not just bare-*handed,*" said Mennofar.

"I had my slingshot," said the boy.

"Bring it forward," said the Duke to his men.

The men glanced at one another awkwardly. Finally, one stepped forward. "Begging your pardon, Your Grace," he said. "We thought it was just an old rag, so we—so it was thrown away."

"Oh, that is too bad," said the Duke in a tone that could never have been mistaken for regretful. "Come along, then. Let's have our little duel."

"Your Majesty, shouldn't His Grace be obliged to provide the, er, the Count of Mossglum with a weapon?" said Just Alice.

Everyone turned and stared at her.

"After all, it was the Duke's retinue that denied him his own," said Just Alice, staring back at all of them.

"That is only fair, Geoffrey," said the King.

The Duke scowled at Just Alice. "I was just about to offer, Your Majesty," he said. He pointed to two of his men. Each one offered the boy the use of his weapon. One had a huge battle-axe. Had both the boy's arms been good, he just might have been able to lift it a few inches off the ground. The other had a longsword that looked only a little more manageable than the axe.

The boy accepted the sword. Just lifting it in the air was enough to make his arm shake. He took a practice swing. The weight of the sword pulled him off balance. He had to take several quick steps just to regain his footing.

A chuckle rolled over the Duke's men.

"This'll do," said the boy.

"And Your Lordship's shield?" said the guard, offering Magan.

The boy looked down at his left arm, hanging uselessly in its sling. "Just the sword, I think," said the boy. "I doubt I'll need anything more." He hoped he sounded braver than he felt.

The Duke smiled and drew his great sword. Its blade

was wider than the boy's arm. It was so heavy that even a man the Duke's size needed both hands to wield it. It glinted in the sun as he took a few practice strokes. "May we have your choice of ground, then?" said the Duke.

The boy stared at the Duke uncertainly.

"I challenged you, so you get to pick where we fight," said the Duke. "There?" He pointed to a spot in the courtyard. "Or there?" He pointed to another. "Or we could go out in front of the palace, if you're more accustomed to fighting in the street." The Duke's men laughed again.

"No, no," said the boy, feigning a bravado he did not really feel. "I choose . . . I choose . . ."

"Mennofar, do something," hissed Just Alice, who had also come out of the crowd.

"The roof," whispered Mennofar. "Choose the roof."

"I choose the roof!" said the boy. He glanced back down at Mennofar and whispered, "Wait, the roof?"

"The roof?" said Just Alice.

"The roof?" said the Duke. "Of the palace?"

Mennofar nodded. "Yes," said the boy, nodding with him. He turned back to the Duke. "The roof of the palace."

Everyone looked up. High above their heads towered a steep pitch of slate shingles. The few remaining gargoyles adorned the edge at odd intervals.

"That's just ridiculous," said the Duke.

"Lord Mossglum does have the choice of ground,"

said the King. "Or not the ground—or whatever." Everyone nodded in agreement, even the Duke's men.

"But he's making a mockery of our duel," spluttered the Duke. He waited a moment before adding, "Your Majesty."

"Your Grace can, of course, forfeit, if you wish," said the King.

"No, no," said the Duke through clenched teeth. "If the boy wishes to die closer to the gods, I shall be happy to accommodate him." He stalked into the main hall of the palace.

"When I said to do something," said Just Alice, "I meant something helpful."

"Thank you for reminding me. I very nearly forgot," said Mennofar. He turned a brighter shade of green and scurried off into the crowd.

♠

Casimir the Merchant stood and watched as his assistants tried without luck to sell his goods. Plenty of townsfolk came to the city market, and most of them stopped at Casimir's stall to take in the aroma of unfamiliar spices or feel the sheerness of real silk. Once they did, though, they moved on to the stalls that sold produce.

"Look at that," he said, and he pointed to the stall across the way. It hummed with housewives buying cheese and eggs.

"They lack the taste necessary to appreciate your wares," said the Factor.

"The vulgar buy silk," said Casimir. "The poor do not. We are wasting our time here."

"I did overhear two of those women gossiping about some duke who apparently has a local princess in his power," said the Factor. "It sounded like a sad tale."

"What do I care about a bunch of infighting nobles in some petty kingdom?" said Casimir.

"It seems he's just arrived at the royal palace," said the Factor, "with an eye to forcing a marriage on her."

"Fool! Why didn't you say something earlier?" said Casimir. Even in a backwater like West Stanhope, it took a good deal of silk to get through a royal wedding. "Move! Move! We must get to the palace right away."

♠

The roof was even steeper than it looked from below. After a long morning in the summer sun, the dark slates were hot, but a life without shoes left the boy with tough feet. He took a couple of experimental steps. The slates were not too slick, but many were loose or broken, or slid beneath his feet. He managed to keep his footing until he glanced down at the courtyard below. The drop made him dizzy. He waved his sword in the air to regain his balance.

At the far end of the roof, the Duke was taking a few

practice swings with his huge sword. When he saw the boy stumble, he smiled. Even though he was dressed in a full suit of chain mail, he strode boldly to the edge. Just watching someone stand so close to the edge made the boy sick, but the Duke was unfazed. He looked down on the crowd below and raised his arms into the air. His men cheered loudly. "When I am done here," he shouted, "I shall order fresh casks of wine to be opened." His men cheered even more loudly. When he stepped back from the lip, a single piece of slate broke loose and slid over the edge. For what seemed like a very long time, it sailed through the air before finally shattering on the flagstones below. An almighty crack echoed back up off the castle walls. The gathered crowd stared at the broken slate for a moment before deciding, as one, to take a few steps back.

The Duke returned to his end of the roof and donned his iron helm.

"Your Grace, are you ready?" cried the King from far below.

"Yes!" shouted the Duke.

"My Lord of Mossglum, are you ready?" cried the King.

"Yes," muttered the boy. He gave the broken link of chain a quick rub for luck.

"Sorry, what?" called the King.

"I said yes," said the boy, a little louder.

The King nodded. The Princess dropped her white handkerchief, and it began.

The Duke charged across the roof without regard for the danger. His footing was sure. The Duke swung his sword at the boy in a heavy arc. Had it connected, it would have cut the boy in half, but without armor, the boy was more nimble than the Duke. He easily darted to one side. The Duke's sword smashed through the roof. An avalanche of slate cascaded down onto the courtyard below.

As he dodged the Duke's attack, the boy managed to deliver a quick blow to the Duke's leg with his sword. Even with all his strength behind the strike, it barely dented the Duke's armor. The boy had hoped it would at least knock him off balance, but that hope went unrewarded. The Duke stood firm.

The boy scurried up to the peak of the roof. The ridge offered him better footing but more directions to fall. He scampered along the ridge to the far end of the roof.

"Come back and die like a man!" shouted the Duke. Before the boy could answer, the Duke charged again. His arm shaking from the weight, the boy raised his sword to block the attack. The Duke batted the boy's sword aside easily. The boy dodged to one side again, but the Duke was prepared. He swung loosely and in such a way that, by shifting his weight suddenly, he could redirect the sword in an unexpected direction without warning. The boy still managed to slip away, but this time it was a close thing indeed. Had the Duke gained an inch or two more, the boy would have lost the top of his skull. Instead, he jumped away as another rain of slate showered down on the courtyard below.

As the boy ducked down and around, he chanced a wild swing at the Duke's ankle. His sword bit only air, but its weight pulled the boy forward off the peak of the roof. He took one big step down the roof. Then another. He knew what was going to happen before it did, but he could do nothing about it. He was too far in front of his own feet. He could not regain his balance.

For a long, heart-stopping moment, he seemed to float above the roof. Then he slammed into the roof face-first. As soon as he landed, he began his headlong slide down. Of its own accord, his bad arm twisted out of the sling and desperately flailed for any grip. The pain was horrible, but it did no good. He did not slow. The edge rushed closer. He ground his nails into the slate tiles, futilely trying to stop his slide.

He went over the edge.

What came next was a wild jumble: He fell. The crowd pointed. Something slammed into him. Sword jerked loose. Couldn't breathe. No air.

That was strange.

There should've been air. It should've been whipping through what was left of his clothing. And the crowd, it should've been looming ever larger in his sight as he drew nearer the ground. Only he wasn't drawing nearer the ground. As the sword clattered on the flagstones far below, the boy's mind congealed around one simple fact: he wasn't falling.

He was, he quickly discovered, clinging to a narrow cornice that had once served as home to one of the absent gargoyles. The boy wasn't sure whether there was a god of cornices, but he gave him a quick prayer of thanksgiving just the same. Then he took a deep breath. Ignoring the pain screaming at him from his bad arm, he spun himself around so that he lay lengthwise along the cornice. He got his feet under him. Getting back up on the roof meant facing the Duke empty-handed, but he did not see what choice he had in the matter. He popped his head up above the edge of the roof.

The Duke had apparently lost his balance, too. He lay on his side with one arm over the ridge. The Duke goggled at the boy. "You have the luck of the Foul One," he wheezed.

The boy only nodded. He jumped onto the roof and ran to the far end from the Duke. The Duke was right, though. He had gotten lucky, that time. There was no reason to think he'd get lucky again. Even if he could keep away from the Duke's sword, he could not keep running back and forth without slipping and falling again. The roof was too steep and too slick for that.

"Maybe not so lucky," said the Duke. "Lost our sword, did we?" He scrambled back to his feet, sending another couple of slates over the edge.

The boy picked up one of the many broken tiles on the roof. He threw it at the Duke as hard as he could. It went well wide of its target.

The Duke snorted. "What are you trying to do? Get me to laugh so hard I fall off the roof?"

The Duke had a point. The boy had nothing, not even the slingshot. The Duke's men had taken the only weapon he actually knew how to use. But it was gone, and—

The boy looked down his front. Slowly, he unlooped the sling Just Alice had made for his bad arm. He knelt down and picked up another broken slate. The best stones were round, not flat like the roof slates, but the boy could make do. He slipped the slate into the sling turned slingshot, gave it a couple of spins over his head and, with a snap of his wrist, let it fly. The stone sailed through the air and struck the Duke's helm with a thunderous clang.

"Now that was annoying," said the Duke, unharmed. "Let us end this, coward!" He began to advance on the boy.

"You're the one who hides behind his title and his men," said the boy. Blood thundered in his ears. "You're the coward."

"What did you say?"

"I said you're the coward."

"What?" said the Duke. "Speak up!" The blow to the helm had deafened him some.

It was the boy's only chance. He took up another

piece of slate, let the slingshot out as far as it would go and spun it around as fast as he could. Then he yelled, "I said you're a—" He dropped his voice to a mumble, then yelled again, "And that your mother is a—" And he dropped his voice again.

"What? How dare you?" said the Duke. "Say that again." The Duke tipped his helm up so he could hear better. When he did, he exposed a corner of his temple.

Hitting a bat midflight with a stone is difficult. Very difficult. But not impossible. With practice, it can be done, and nothing spurs practice like hunger. During all those months in the Spine, the boy had gotten lots of practice, and when he failed, his empty belly had spurred him to practice more. Even though the Duke's temple was a very small target, and even though the Duke exposed it only briefly, it was nowhere near as hard to hit as a bat in flight.

The boy snapped his wrist so hard he thought his hand might come off. The stone ripped through the air and landed with a sound a little like a kiss.

♠

It was a good strike, but the blow itself was not fatal. That much the Duke knew. His head swam a little, so he blinked a few times and then shook his head to clear his vision. He did not begin to worry until he took a stagger-step forward. Suddenly he could not seem to keep his body over his feet. His stomach lurched sickeningly as he stumbled faster and faster down the face of the roof. He managed, just in time, to steer himself toward one of the gargoyles. He slammed into it, hard. The gargoyle knocked the wind from him, but it stopped him cold. Gasping and sweating, he clung to the ugly statue. "Good try, lad, but not good enough," he shouted. "I'll not make that mistake again."

The truly awful part was that when the truth came to him, it came just a little too late. Were it not for the ringing in his ears, he might have heard the creaking sound of ancient masonry giving way, of the gargoyle freeing itself from its anchor. Had he heard that creaking sound, he might have scrambled back onto the roof in time.

But the Duke did not hear. He did not realize what was happening until the gargoyle began to move. Man and gargoyle pitched forward into the air. The Duke watched the ground rush toward him. It was not right. This was not how it was supposed to end. He had plans. He was to be king. He wanted to protest, but all he could do was choke out a strangled "I—I—" before the gargoyle's flight came to an abrupt end on the flagstones below.

17

When the boy returned to the courtyard, there was nothing to be done for Duke Geoffrey. One of his men draped the Duke's cloak over him. The rest just stood there, fussing uselessly.

"You've slain the Duke," said the King. He beamed at the boy. "The whole kingdom owes you a debt of gratitude."

"The Roofers' Guild particularly," said the Minister of the Treasury as he surveyed the damage to the palace.

"I am the one in your debt," said the Princess. She

took the boy's hand in hers. "That's the second time you've saved me."

"And now you don't have to marry someone just because he's rich and has an army," said the boy.

"Ah, yes, er, umm, yes," said the King. "About that . . ."

The Queen forced a smile onto her face. "Darling, you remember your third cousin Prince Edgar, don't you?"

"A charming young man," said the Steward helpfully.

"And what he lacks in chin, he makes up for in nose," said the Tipstaff, less helpfully.

"Perhaps we might focus on more immediate matters, Your Majesty," said the Chamberlain in a low tone. "As there are some issues that are, as yet, unaddressed." He paused to make sure they all followed him. When he saw they did not, he added, "The Duke's men."

The Duke might have been dead, but his many soldiers were not. The greater portion of the armed forces of West Stanhope were milling around, leaderless and freshly unemployed.

"Oh, dear," said the King. He looked to the Chamberlain, but the Chamberlain only pursed his lips with worry.

"None of you have any idea what to do?" asked the Princess.

The members of the cabinet all looked down at their feet. A few of them gave little shrugs.

Princess Alice marched to the top of the steps, held her head high and, in her most regal voice, said, "Men of Castle Geoffrey, I, Alice, Crown Princess of West Stanhope and All Its Dependencies, have grave news to impart. Unbeknownst to you all, your late master, Duke Geoffrey, was secretly plotting against me and against my father, the King." She gave her father a nod. "This vile malefactor is dead now, slain by my personal champion"—here she pointed at the boy—"and his evil schemes are defeated. I'm sure that none of you knew anything about this treasonous conspiracy against the Crown." She paused to let the Duke's men tell one another that they had, in fact, known nothing about any treason. "For you are all loyal subjects of the King." Another pause let them reassure one another of their loyalty to the King. "And in recognition of your loyalty, my father will stand as your host at any inn or tavern in the city."

There was a long pause as the Duke's men considered her words. Finally, one of the men-at-arms said, "Not to sound ungracious, Your Highness, but just how many drinks are we talking about?"

The Princess looked him squarely in the eye and said, "As many as you want! Father will pay for them all!" The Minister of the Treasury did some quick calculations and then went very pale.

"Three cheers for the Princess!" shouted the man-at-arms. The Duke's men shouted, "Hurrah for Princess Alice! Hurrah for Princess Alice! Hurrah for Princess

Alice!" Cheering and shouting, the men poured out of the palace courtyard.

"There," said the Princess. "That's how to sort them out."

"Well done," said the King. He hoisted her up in his arms. "Worthy of a monarch. Truly."

The Princess blushed, and giggled just a little.

The King put the Princess back down. "Now, tell me what really happened."

The Princess launched into a breathless, and somewhat garbled, account of how the boy had bested an ogre, freed Just Alice, faced down the dragon and freed Princess Alice, all before exposing the treachery of Duke Geoffrey and slaying him in single combat. She didn't even slow down when she came to the part of the story that the King had seen for himself.

"You did all that?" said the King.

"Um, I guess I did, Your Majesty," said the boy.

"Very impressive, young man," said the King.

"I always saw a lot of promise in the lad, myself," said the Earl. He clamped his hand down firmly on the boy's shoulder. "That's why I made him my personal champion and charged him with rescuing the Princess."

The boy jumped a little at that.

"You did?" said the King.

"Of course, Your Majesty," said the Earl. "How else could he have gotten hold of Magan—my *personal* shield? Right, lad?"

"Absolutely right," said the boy, nodding vigorously.

"Well done, Godric," said the King. "For that, I shall make you Marquis of—"

The Queen elbowed him. "Duke," she whispered just loud enough for everyone to hear.

"*Duke* of Middlebury."

"Thank you, Your Majesty," said the newly appointed duke, bowing deeply.

"And what about you, lad?" said the King. "You must have a reward, too. As I'm making Godric here a duke, would you like to be an earl?"

♠

Casimir was stuck behind the crowd at the palace gates. He craned his neck to look into the courtyard, but all he could see was a sea of heads. Then a great cheer went up. "What is it?" he said. "What's going on?"

"It's the Duke," said someone standing nearby. "He's dead."

"Dead? How?" said Casimir.

"He's thrown himself from the top of a tall tower because the King refused his proposal."

"No, he was slain by a foreign assassin," said someone else. "Stabbed him right in the back."

"I heard he lost a duel with a beggar," said a third.

"But the wedding's definitely off?" said the Factor.

"Oh, yes," said the first man. "No groom."

Casimir cursed and spat.

There was a tug at the hem of his coat. "Casimir the Merchant, I am Mennofar the Goblin. I believe we have a little business to transact."

There, at Casimir's feet, in violation of all sense and reason, stood a goblin. A lesser man—a lesser merchant—might have stood and gawped at such a sight, but the goblin had mentioned business. That was enough for Casimir. "It is a great pleasure to meet you, Mennofar the Goblin," he said in his silkiest tone. The situation required care. Goblins were well known for sharp practice. "You are very fortunate to catch me, for I carry only the finest wares in all of the Kingdoms, and my visit to Farnham is but a brief one."

"And yet, one I have been looking forward to for many months," said Mennofar.

"Many months?" said the Factor. "But we only decided to come here last—"

"Let us not quibble over trivial matters," said Casimir. If Mennofar wanted to think he knew where Casimir was going before Casimir did, let him. Goblins had gold. That was the important thing. "Now, what sort of business were you interested in transacting?"

"You have lost something, and I thought I might reunite you with it," said Mennofar, his skin glowing a brilliant shade of green.

"I'm intrigued, I will admit that," said Casimir. He stroked the end of his great black mustache. "But I'll not commit to a reward until I have my property back, whatever it may be."

"Fair enough," said Mennofar. He smiled, exposing his hundreds of pointy little teeth. "Follow me."

♠

King Julian's offer to make the boy an earl might have sounded offhanded, but it was not. He dangled this prize in the hopes that the boy might take it over the Princess's hand. The kingdom was still broke, even more so now that it had a large bar tab to pick up. King Julian still needed the Princess to marry a rich prince.

The boy said, "Thank you, Your Majesty, but no. I've been thinking about the reward and—"

"Of course, the Princess's hand in marriage is the traditional reward in such circumstances." He estimated the boy's age. "Perhaps a long engagement? Say, two years?" Then, very awkwardly, he added, "Son."

"Again, very generous, Your Majesty, but I wasn't going to ask for that, either," said the boy.

"Gold, then?" said King Julian. For if the boy did not want a title or the Princess's hand, then he had to want money, and a great deal of it. Certainly more than the kingdom had.

"No, Your Highness. For my boon, I ask that you abolish slavery in West Stanhope," said the boy.

The members of the court gasped, but King Julian did not immediately refuse. This royal silence made the Chamberlain nervous. "Your Majesty is not, I hope, seriously considering this?" he said.

"Oh, Papa, you must," said Princess Alice. "I've been learning all about slavery, and it is ever so nasty."

"Her Highness has a delicate and sensitive nature, as is only proper for a princess," soothed the Bailiff. "But exposure to luridly exaggerated accounts of the harsher aspects of this particular institution"—he squinted at the boy—"may have overcome her natural faculties of logic and reason."

"You make it sound as though I've gone soft," said Princess Alice. "Why shouldn't Papa outlaw slavery?"

"But it's . . . it's . . . *unprecedented,*" spluttered the Bailiff.

"Your Majesty, as a sage, I feel obliged to point out that there is a precedent," said Oswald. "The Bergstad Federation abolished slavery over a hundred years ago."

"And we are supposed to embrace every new fad just because it strikes the fancy of some foreign land?" cried the Tipstaff indignantly. "Undermining the very fabric of our society and abandoning our great Stanhoptic traditions?"

"And will abolishing slavery create a security risk?" said the Captain of the Guard. "What's to stop these newly freed slaves from taking up arms against the state?"

"What, exactly, stops them from doing that now?" asked Just Alice.

The Captain of the Guard glared at her.

"I think Your Majesty must consider the legal questions here," said the Seneschal. "I fear this issue may not fall within Your Majesty's jurisdiction. It may be a matter best suited for the High King in—"

"Your Majesty, what about the job losses?" interrupted the Minister of the Treasury. "If you abolish slavery, then the slaves will all be thrown out of work."

"I fear that Your Majesty's natural desire to help these poor unfortunates can only serve to make their lives worse," said the Steward.

"How would freeing them make their lives worse?" demanded Just Alice.

That earned her an imperious glare from the Steward. "These people have no experience of being free," he said. "If you just free them willy-nilly, they will lack the skills to care for themselves. Now, if we were to wait, say, five years—"

"They'd be just as unprepared as they are today," said Princess Alice.

"It's a tragic situation," agreed the Steward. "They may never be ready."

It was plain that the cabinet had not scored as many points as they had hoped. In desperation, they all looked to the Chamberlain to save them. For a long moment, everyone remained silent as the Chamberlain considered what to say. Finally, he laced his fingers together and cracked all of his knuckles at once, then took a deep breath.

"Better make it a good one," said the Princess.

The Chamberlain took an even deeper breath, bowed slightly to the King and said, "As Your Majesty can see, this particular institution, while perhaps somewhat distasteful, is part of a complex web of interconnected social institutions. And while it is only natural to feel a certain sympathy for the less fortunate, this web should not be disturbed lightly. Under the circumstances, an extended study by a committee of sages—a committee I would be only too happy to organize for Your Majesty—would permit a more complete understanding of the role of this particular institution in our society. This understanding would help us to develop a scheme for dismantling it, or perhaps simply reforming it so as to curtail certain excesses, should that prove the wiser course. And if, in the meantime, this puts some small few in awkward circumstances, I am confident that they can rely on the benevolence of their betters to improve their individual situations."

When it was clear that the Chamberlain was done, the officers of the royal cabinet all clapped and said, "Hear, hear." There was even a smattering of applause from some members of the crowd. The Chamberlain bowed a little in acknowledgment.

The King, however, said nothing. He simply stared off into space.

"Your Majesty?" said the Chamberlain.

"Hmm? What?" said the King, snapping out of it. "Sorry, I was miles away."

While his ministers fussed about what would happen if he granted the boy's request, King Julian worried about what might happen if he refused. There was little chance that West Stanhope would be able to afford the boy's second choice, whatever it might be. And there were not so very many slaves in West Stanhope, mostly because the people of West Stanhope lacked the kind of wealth to afford things like slaves. Granting the boy's request would put a few noses out of joint, but—and this was key—it would not actually cost any money.

"My lords, ladies and gentlemen," said King Julian in his most regal tone. "My ministers have spoken eloquently in defense of our great Stanhoptic traditions." The ministers and other members of the court nodded vigorously in support of King Julian's words. "I will not let it be said that I violated our most ancient tradition"—he paused for effect—"of granting a hero any boon that is within my power. Therefore, I am outlawing slavery in West Stanhope immediately. Bailiff, prepare a decree to be read in every town and village in the land."

The Chamberlain clenched his teeth, but the crowd cheered King Julian's decree. A few of them cheered because they were genuinely opposed to slavery. The rest cheered because they preferred dramatic royal proclamations over getting back to work.

"Hurrah," cried Princess Alice, who was one of the few genuinely excited by King Julian's decree. "Well done, Papa!"

♠

Mennofar sliced through the crowd with surprising speed, but Casimir managed to keep up. They quickly came to the front.

"I believe you know *him,*" said Mennofar, pointing.

"Who would I know in Farnham?" said Casimir, but the boy Mennofar pointed to *was* familiar. He was definitely one of Casimir's slaves, although Casimir could not say exactly which one. There were so very, very many. And how one of them had wound up in Farnham was a mystery. Still, there would be time enough to sort that out after he reclaimed his property.

He crept up on the boy slowly and with great care. Then, when he was close enough, he struck like a viper. He caught the boy by the wrist, taking him by surprise. "I have you now, slave!"

18

The hold on his wrist felt more like an iron shackle than a man's grasp. The boy looked up. "Mast— Casimir," he said.

At the name, Just Alice squealed and threw her hands over her mouth.

"Abase yourself before your master, slave," said Casimir. The boy felt the pull of habit tugging his forehead toward the ground.

"No," said the boy. He drew himself up to his full height.

Casimir squeezed the boy's wrist still harder. His nails bit into the boy's skin. "Boy—"

The Factor stumbled out of the crowd. "Very sorry, sir." He wheezed and gasped for air. "Hard to keep up at my age."

"Never mind that," said Casimir. "Pay the goblin a florin. He has returned a renegade slave to us."

"Really," said the Factor. "Which one?"

Casimir scowled. "Shut up and give the goblin his reward."

The boy watched the Factor take out a florin and drop it into Mennofar's open hands.

The boy felt sick. After all they had been through together, he thought Mennofar was a friend. But Mennofar had warned him that a goblin and a human could not truly be friends.

For his part, Mennofar did not even have the decency to be embarrassed. He smiled at the boy as if nothing were wrong at all. Indeed, he almost seemed to be expecting the boy to do something.

"Papa, that man is kidnapping, er, the boy who rescued me! Do something!" cried the Princess.

"What, exactly, do you think you are doing?" the King asked Casimir.

Casimir bowed deeply without letting go of the boy's wrist. "Please forgive the interruption, Your Majesty," he simpered. "It is a simple matter. This boy is my slave, and I am merely reclaiming him. With your leave, I shall be happy to absent myself."

"Don't be ridiculous," said the King. "That young

man is a hero of the kingdom. And the Count of Mossglum. Release him at once."

"With respect, Your Majesty, Gergo, Count of Mossglum, is very nearly eighty years old and missing one eye," said Casimir. "Through my business dealings in High Albemarle, I am slightly acquainted with His Lordship." Casimir turned a contemptuous eye on the boy. "The real one, I mean."

"Is this true?" said the King.

It was an excellent moment for a really well-timed lie.

"Uh," said the boy. "Um—"

"I see," said the King. "Nevertheless, the boy is still a hero of the kingdom. Besides, there are no slaves in West Stanhope. I, personally, have outlawed slavery this very day."

Casimir gasped in shock but quickly recovered. "Your Majesty is very forward-thinking, to be sure," he said. "Regrettably, as I am a subject of High Albemarle, not West Stanhope, your new laws, while no doubt wise and progressive, don't apply to me. Or my property." He gave the boy's wrist a shake. "I'm sure Your Majesty has some legal scholar who can confirm this."

The King looked to the Seneschal.

"Without the authorization of the High King, Your Majesty's laws can only apply to Your Majesty's subjects," said the Seneschal. "An awkward technicality, under the circumstances, but one well established in the law."

"I see," said the King. He looked to the boy. "Is this

true, son? Are you the slave of this High Albemarlian? Or is it High Albemarlmite?"

"If it please Your Majesty, it is Albemarlman," said Casimir.

"Albemarlman, then," said the King. "Are you the slave of this High Albemarlman?"

"No," said the boy. His traitor voice quavered.

Casimir's black eyes glittered with rage. "Keep it up, slave, and I'll have that tongue for a paperweight," he whispered into the boy's ear.

"This boy is a hero," said the King. "He defeated an ogre and a dragon, and he rescued two maidens, one of whom was my daughter. His word is good enough for me."

"Oh, how it pains me to tell you that his word is not, as Your Majesty so eloquently put it, good enough," said Casimir.

"Don't talk rot," said the King.

"Sadly, when making a petition for liberty on the grounds of wrongful enslavement," said Casimir, "the petitioner may not personally give evidence of his condition."

"What in the name of the Foul One does that mean?" said the King.

"It means that he"—Casimir shook the boy for emphasis—"may not speak to whether he is a slave. It is an ancient law."

The King looked to the Seneschal, who looked away. "Another awkward technicality," said the Seneschal.

"That's ridiculous," said the Princess. "Why shouldn't he be allowed to tell us whether he's a slave?"

"Your Highness, you are innocent and naïve, as is only proper for a princess," said Casimir. "I hesitate to point out that a slave, being selfish and dishonest as all slaves are, might—*just might*—lie to get out of his duties."

"As opposed to a slave owner, who, being selfless and honorable as all slave owners are, would never—*never*—lie to get a free slave," said Just Alice.

Casimir scowled at her and twisted the end of his great black mustache. "Others may testify." He looked her up and down. "You, for example. Can you swear that he is not my slave?"

Just Alice looked away.

"How about the rest of you?" said Casimir. "Can any of you swear that he is not my slave?"

The King looked to Princess Alice. She looked to Oswald, who looked to the Duke of Middlebury, who then looked to the Queen. The Queen turned to the King as the ministers all looked off into the distance. The silence grew longer. And more painful.

"Papa, do something," said Princess Alice. She began to weep.

"This is unjust," said Just Alice.

"The sadnesses of this life are many," said Casimir. "But the most bitter is that nothing is more elusive than justice." He began to pull the boy toward his ship. "We are leaving, slave."

The boy dug his heels into the ground. "I'm not a slave!" he shouted, as though he could make it true by saying it forcefully enough.

Casimir smiled cruelly. "Can you prove it?" he said.

"Yes." Mennofar turned to the boy. "Can *you* prove it?"

Mennofar might have betrayed him, but he no longer smiled or looked expectant. He actually looked quite worried. His skin had gone an inky green darker than any the boy had ever seen.

"Can you prove it here in Farnham?" said Mennofar.

Months ago, Mennofar had told the boy that Farnham was the only place in the world where he had any chance of proving he was not a slave. It was the reason he had walked all the way to West Stanhope. Of course, it all made more sense back when he thought he was not a slave. Now that he knew better, it made none. So it was impossible to prove that he was not a slave, because he *was* one. Then again, Mennofar had sworn to tell the truth when he said that proving it was possible. So it was also impossible that it was impossible to prove he was not a slave. Everything was impossible. It was the sort of nonsense that Mennofar loved, but it just made the boy dizzy.

And back when the boy rescued him, Mennofar hadn't wanted to give Casimir a vow. Yet he had betrayed the boy to Casimir anyway, which guaranteed that Casimir would get Mennofar's last vow. That also made no sense. Only it probably would make sense in some inside-out kind of way. Everything Mennofar did was like that. It was maddening how—

"He has a witness," said Just Alice.

"I do?" said the boy. "Er, I mean, yes, I do." He looked at the gathered crowd, trying to think who might be able to lie for him. "Who is it?" he whispered.

"Mennofar the Goblin," said Just Alice.

"Yes!" said the boy. "Mennofar the Goblin!" No one he knew was a better liar.

"A goblin? Testifying?" said Casimir. "Absurd. Out of the question."

"He's quite right," said the Seneschal. "They are tricksome deceivers. Ancient law prohibits them from giving testimony under any circumstances."

"I should hope so," said Mennofar indignantly.

"Even if he vowed to tell the truth?" said Just Alice.

Casimir turned ever so slightly pale at the suggestion. "Er, makes no difference," he said quickly. "Come along, now." He tugged at the boy's arm.

"Did I say 'under any circumstances'?" said the Seneschal. "I may have spoken too hastily."

Casimir sighed. "Very well," he said. "If you can extract a vow to tell the truth from this ridiculous creature, go right ahead." He smiled tightly at Just Alice.

"I can't," she said. She pointed to the boy. "He can."

That would be no help at all. All Mennofar could say was: *Yes, the boy is your slave, but slavery is a great injustice. So would you, out of the goodness of your heart, pretty please, let him go anyway?* Casimir did not care if slavery was unjust. He had hundreds of slaves, and the boy doubted if Casimir had ever even given the question of justice a moment's thought.

The boy stopped. He turned and looked straight into Casimir's cold, dark eyes.

"What?" snarled Casimir.

The boy jerked his arm from Casimir's grasp. "Mennofar the Goblin, you owe this man a vow. Please tell him what you told me the day we met."

Mennofar smiled back toothily. His skin shone emerald green. "Casimir the Merchant, I, Mennofar the Goblin, vow that this one thing I am about to tell you is true: this boy is not truly and justly a slave."

Casimir never did figure it out, not even years later. For him, the world was a simple place. Some men were meant to rule, and the rest were slaves. He never doubted which of the two he was supposed to be. Indeed, he never even thought to wonder. It never, ever occurred to him that the boy might have slipped his grasp on the word "justly" alone.

Instead, he assumed that he had been cheated. As he could not remember exactly which of his slaves the boy was, he could not quite remember how he had come to own him. But he easily could have bought the boy from someone who had stolen him or seized him on false pretenses. It happened to poor children all the time. In truth, Casimir did not especially care. Important men had slaves, so he deserved as many as he could get. And if it turned out that, because of some legal technicality, a few of them were not actually supposed to be slaves, he could live with it.

At least, he could live with it if he could get away with it. But in this case, he could not. The King was plainly eager to see the boy free and was sure to accept the goblin's vow. Worse, the boy might demand retribution from his false master. Casimir might have been greedy, heartless, calculating, dishonest, cruel and vain, but he was not stupid. He knew when to cut his losses.

He threw himself on the ground and began to weep bitterly. "Oh, the unfairness, the injustice of it all," he cried out.

"You're hardly the victim here," said the King.

"I?" said Casimir. "I do not weep for myself, Your Majesty. It is the tragic tale of this poor boy that brings me to tears."

"You— Wait, what?" said the King.

"This poor, poor boy, wrongly bound and fraudulently presented to me, an innocent and deceived buyer, as a slave," said Casimir. "He labors for years in ignominy. Can you fathom the horror of it?"

"I am on the verge of tears, myself," said the Factor drily.

"Oh, poor, sweet, tragic child, can you ever forgive me?" sobbed Casimir, grasping the boy's ankle.

"Um, er, um," said the boy.

Mennofar coughed a little. "Did I hear that right? *You* are innocent?"

Casimir rose to his knees. "Goblin, know that I had no idea this boy was not a slave. I truly believed him to legally be my personal property. Indeed, you who know all, can you vow otherwise?"

"Well," said Mennofar. "No."

"Then can you forgive me, boy?" said Casimir.

Before the boy could reply, Mennofar said, "What of compensation?"

Casimir smiled tightly. "Yes, of course," he said. "I will pay compensation in the amount of ten—"

"One hundred," said Mennofar.

"Fifteen?" said Casimir.

"Eighty-five."

"Twenty-five?"

"Seventy."

"Thirty?"

"Sixty."

"Forty?"

"Fifty."

"Done," said Casimir. He turned to the boy. "*Now* do you forgive me?" he snapped.

♠

"Yes," said the boy. Fifty hellers of copper was a tidy sum, enough to start a young man out in the world. And he wanted the whole business settled before anyone thought to start asking questions. "Of course I forgive you."

Casimir nodded to the Factor. The Factor opened his purse and began counting out coins. The boy goggled as the Factor put not copper hellers but silver florin after silver florin into the boy's outstretched hands. Each florin was worth twenty hellers. When the Factor was done, the boy's hands were filled with silver. In The Tales, a fortune was always a sack of *gold*. But the boy did not care. He always called this a fortune.

Casimir put his arm around the boy's shoulder, leaned in and whispered in the boy's ear, "You're a clever lad, all right, and your friend is cleverer still. If I ever catch you in High Albemarle, you'll spend the rest of your very short life in the silver mines." Turning to the King, he said, "If Your Majesty would be so kind as to excuse me, I find myself tempted by the next tide."

"Yes, of course, you are dismissed," said the King. Under his breath, he added, "And we're well shot of you." He said it just loudly enough that everyone had to pretend they didn't hear him.

Once Casimir and the Factor left, everyone crowded in to congratulate the boy. The Queen smiled at him. Both Oswald and the Duke of Middlebury clapped the boy on the shoulder. The Princess kissed him on the cheek. The boy's face reddened, while Just Alice glared at her.

Then the King cleared his throat, and everyone took a step back. The boy looked up at the King and said, "Your Majesty, about that Count of Mossglum business, I just—"

"*Permuddlare necesse est,* young man," said the King quietly, and he tapped the side of his nose. *"Permuddlare necesse est."*

"Er, yes, exactly," said the boy. As he had no idea what the King was talking about, it was the best response he could manage.

The King leaned forward to whisper in the boy's ear. "I don't think we'll be seeing him again," said the King. "So if you want to change your mind and pick a different boon, I'd allow it."

The boy gave it a moment's thought. That was quite an offer. He could become a lord and rule over his lands from his castle. It would be a big step up for someone born a slave. But there were other slaves in West Stanhope. "No, thank you, Your Majesty," he said. "I'm fine the way I am."

The King gave the boy a hearty thump on the back. "Good lad." He turned to the crowd and said, "What, no cheers for—" He turned back to the boy. "What is your real name?"

"I haven't got one," said the boy.

The King turned back to the crowd. "No cheers for our young hero?"

"Hurrah for Hero!" cried the assembled crowd.

"Wait," said the boy. "You're saying it wrong."

But the crowd ignored him. "Hurrah for Hero!" they cried again.

"How's it wrong?" said Just Alice.

"They're calling me Hero like it's my name," said the boy. "But it's not."

"Hurrah for Hero!" cried the crowd a third time.

"I don't know," said Just Alice. "Isn't your name just whatever people call you?"

"Hero is a stupid name," said Hero.

"Nobody likes their name," said Just Alice. "Not really."

Hero looked out at the crowd of onlookers smiling at him. He turned to Mennofar and said, "I'm stuck with it, aren't I?"

Mennofar smiled and turned a particularly vibrant shade of emerald. "I think you will find that I am under no obligation to answer that question," he said. "Or any other, for that matter." But Hero did not need Mennofar's answer. He already knew it was too late to do anything about it.

19

The Great Hall of the Council of Sages sat on a hill overlooking Roggenheim's busy port. The first forty of Hero's florins had gone to pay the debts on Oswald's farm, for which Oswald made Hero his partner in the farm. Another nine florins went for seed and tools, making the farm productive and successful for the first time. But the fiftieth had gone so Just Alice could come to Roggenheim and plead her case to the Council in person.

Hero and Oswald sat in the front row of the gallery as Just Alice stood before the Council. In his last visit, Mennofar had given her a lot of advice on how to address the Council. She reminded herself to do the opposite of everything he said. He was a goblin, after all. Hero had given her his ring to wear around her neck for luck. She gave it a quick rub before she began, and then she told the Council her story. It was a slow day, and her voice echoed through the nearly empty hall. Still, she did a good job of telling the tale, or so she thought. She even managed to be a little humble, at least sometimes. When she was done, no one said a word for a long moment. The five members of the Council stroked their long white beards and vaguely hoped that one of the others would speak first. Finally, Egbert of Roggenheim said, "Why not grant her the extraordinary? How long's it been since we gave one out, anyway?"

"Not nearly long enough, if anyone were to ask me, which, I note, no one did," said Old Henry. He squinted at Egbert nearsightedly. Even by the standard of the Council of Sages, Old Henry was a very old man. Indeed, he had been *Old* Henry long enough to bury more than one Young Henry. "And I'm not sure I approve of such a cavalier approach to a matter as serious as this, young man." There were nods and murmurs of agreement with this.

"Well, I'm not sure I approve of one member of the Council upbraiding another in public," said Egbert. He crossed his arms. There were nods and murmurs of agreement with this, too.

♠

In the gallery, Hero whispered to Oswald, "It doesn't seem to be going well."

"It's always like this," Oswald whispered back. "Sages like to bicker."

"I vote yes," said Egbert.

"He was always a safe vote," whispered Oswald. "He and I both apprenticed for the same master."

"I think we should consider abolishing extraordinaries altogether," said Old Henry. "There's a danger of corruption. Those with the right connections could influence the process."

"Unlike agon invitations, which are always issued with the purest of motives," said Just Alice. Hero winced a little at that.

Old Henry peered down his long nose at Just Alice. "The impertinence!" he snapped. "Young lady, you will speak only when asked a question."

"Yes, sir. Sorry, sir," said Just Alice.

"She's far too contrary to be a sage," said Old Henry. "I vote no."

"Aren't all sages contrary?" said Egbert.

"No!" snapped Old Henry. "And don't you start in with the impertinence."

"Don't worry, we never had a chance with him," whispered Oswald. "He votes no on everything."

"I have a different concern," said Roderick of Clontarf. "I was a little confused by your story, but if I understand it right, this boy really was a slave."

"Yes, sir," said Just Alice.

"And you helped to get his master to renounce any claim on him by means of, well, of a sort of trick, I suppose," said Roderick.

"I guess you could call it that," said Just Alice, "but—"

"Then, by your own admission, you basically cheated an honest man out of something that belonged to him," said Roderick. "We require the highest standards of honesty and ethical conduct in our profession." He scowled at Just Alice. "I vote no."

"That's bad," whispered Oswald.

"These things can be complicated," said Walter of Uskborough. "Under the circumstances—" He waved King Julian's letter of recommendation in the air.

"Impertinence!" snapped Old Henry. "No, wait, I meant influence." He pointed at the letter. "Influence!"

"—I vote yes."

"So it's down to me," said Alfred the Gray. He sat and considered it for a long moment. "It's a goblin's puzzle. There's just no arguing with that," he said at last, and he shrugged. "By a vote of three to two, an extraordinary is awarded to the girl known as Just Alice. Young lady, if you can find a sage to take you on, you may apprentice yourself to him."

"Thank you," said Just Alice, bowing her head a little.

She turned and rushed over to Hero and Oswald. They both rose to meet her. "Outside, quickly, before someone changes his mind," she whispered.

The three of them slipped out of the Great Hall. Once they were out in the bustling streets of Roggenheim, Oswald gave her a big hug. "Congratulations, my dear," said Oswald.

"Thank you, Papa," she said.

Hero hugged her as well. "You were great up there," he said.

"Of course I was," she said, but she smiled a little. "Luckily, enough of them saw that."

"Don't think I missed Alfred's little dig," said Oswald. " '*If* you can find a sage'? Really."

"Are you still going to let me be your apprentice?" said Just Alice.

"Of course I will," said Oswald. "I didn't mean—"

"Then it doesn't matter what he said," said Just Alice.

Oswald nodded. "Quite right. Quite right."

"The tide is still with us," said Hero. "If we are quick, we can sail for Farnham today." He took Just Alice by the hand and led her down the street.

"Come on, Papa, come on," called Just Alice over her shoulder as she and Hero hurried, hand in hand, toward the ship that would take them all home.

AFTERWORD

Dear Reader,

Now that you've read *The Goblin's Puzzle,* you know that a lot of the story has to do with logical puzzles, errors and fallacies. (And if you haven't read the book, why have you skipped to the end to read the afterword first? Is there something wrong with you?) Anyway, by the end of the book, most of the logical twists and turns have been explained. But there's still that business with the boy convincing Ludwig he is "no one."

I'd like to take a moment to explain just how wrong the boy was and why, but first you need to know a few things about **logic.** Logic is the study of how we prove things. In logic, you have **premises** and **conclusions.** A premise is an idea we assume to be true. When you put a couple of premises together, they might lead you to discover something new: a conclusion. Taken together, the premises and conclusion add up to an **argument,** but not the kind you have with your little brother (and stop picking on him). A famous example goes like this:

> *All men are mortal. Socrates is a man.*
> *Therefore, Socrates is mortal.*

"All men are mortal" and "Socrates is a man" are your premises. If they are true, then your conclusion—"Socrates is mortal"—must also be true. That's the case here, so the argument is valid. (Socrates, by the way, was an ancient Greek philosopher who was famous for asking awkward questions. Eventually, everyone got sick of this and he was executed. So he was definitely mortal. And if *you* like asking awkward questions, let that be a lesson to you.)

When the conclusion is true *because* the premises are true, the argument is **valid.** The premises prove the conclusion. Our "Socrates is mortal" argument, for example, is valid. But be careful. It is not enough that your premises and conclusion all happen to be true. The premises must cause your conclusion to be true. Consider, for a moment, a slightly different argument:

All men are mortal. Socrates is mortal.
Therefore, Socrates is a man.

That might sound good, but it isn't valid. To see why, try substituting "my dog Scout" for "Socrates." You get: "All men are mortal." True. "My dog Scout is mortal." Also true. (Sorry, boy.) "Therefore, my dog Scout is a man." Oops. The argument is invalid because it embraces a **fallacy**—an error in logical reasoning. In this case, the argument makes the mistake of suggesting that because all men are mortal, all mortal creatures must be men. This particular fallacy is called **mistaking the part for the whole.**

Now, let's take a look at the boy's argument in chapter 11:

No one has no name. I have no name.
Therefore, I am no one.

Just Alice shows us that the boy is mistaking the part for the whole. But there is something even more wrong with the boy's argument. In fact, the boy piles several different fallacies on top of each other. Another of his fallacies—as Just Alice points out—is **reification.** Reification is the fallacy of treating something abstract or intangible as if it were a solid object.

Love is more precious than gold. You should keep precious things in a safe. Therefore, you should keep love in a safe.

In the same way, the boy uses the phrase "no one" as if there were such a person. That's reification.

But there's at least one more fallacy that the boy uses—**equivocation.** Equivocation is when you use the same word or phrase to mean different things at different times. A good example of equivocation is:

The water is full of man-eating sharks. Brenda is not a man. Therefore, it should be safe for Brenda to take a dip.

The first time we use the word "man"—"man-eating sharks"—we use it to mean human beings. (A bit sexist, but there it is.) The second time—"Brenda is not a man"—we use it to mean males. And so it is in the boy's argument to the dragon. The first time the boy uses "no one," he means "There is no such person." That's how he gets the dragon to agree with the statement. But the second time he uses "no one," he means—well, it's not exactly clear what he means, but he seems to mean that there is a particular person "no one," kind of like there is a particular dragon "Ludwig."

(If, by the way, you are unusually clever, you might have noticed that our man-eating-shark argument also used the fallacy of mistaking the part for the whole. After all, my dog Scout is not a man by any definition, but I suspect he would be no better off swimming with those man-eating sharks than poor Brenda. Fallacies, it turns out, are a bit like man-eating sharks. They'll sneak up on you if you let them.)

To see what's really wrong with the boy's argument, try rephrasing the first premise. If you think about it, "No one has no name" really means the same thing as "Everyone has a name." Swap those two out, and the boy's argument becomes:

> *Everyone has a name. I have no name.*
> *Therefore—*

Uh-oh.

Remember that a valid argument is one where the conclusion must be true when both of the premises are true. In this case, the two premises contradict each other. They cannot both be true at the same time. The boy cannot use these two premises to construct any valid argument.

But, I hear you cry, *the boy did free Ludwig. If his argument was invalid, how could he do that?*

Well, even when an argument is invalid, the conclusion can still turn out to be true. Think back to "All men are mortal. Socrates is mortal. Therefore, Socrates is a man." The argument is invalid, but Socrates really *is* a man. The conclusion is still true. In fact, arguing that a conclusion is false because the argument that supports that conclusion is invalid is itself a logical fallacy. It is called, somewhat imaginatively, the **fallacy fallacy.**

But all of this does not quite answer the question of how the boy was able to free Ludwig. How does he have this power? Where does it come from? I'm afraid I'm going to leave that to you to work out on your own. I can't do everything for you. Well, maybe I can, but I'm not going to. After all, where would the fun be in that?

Your friend,
Andrew S. Chilton

ACKNOWLEDGMENTS

I owe a great debt to the many, many people whose help made this book possible. Thanks first to the thaumaturges: Pam Howell, my agent, and Katherine Harrison, my editor. In addition, this book would almost certainly never have been published without the indispensable help of John Claude Bemis and Dante W. Harper. Then there are all those who gave me so much advice, encouragement and help along the way, always, it seemed, at just the right moment. These include Greg and Karen Wilson, Matt Stiegler, Patty Skuster, Chris Quinn, Joan Petit, Kami Patterson, James McDonald, Chris Marthinson, Chris Lee, Mike Jones, Jack Hott, Kerry-Anne Harris, Paul Hamilton, Jody Grant, Joe Gomez, Erin Galli, Preston Dunlop, Jennifer Drolet, Helen Cox, Mark Chilton, Ted Blaszak, David Auerbach, Miriam Angress and Fatima Alejos-Gonzalez. Doubtless, there are many more who are slipping my mind. To them, I can only say, "Oops."